"Deal," he said, holding out his hand

"You make ten thousand dollars by Mardi Gras—and you win. One penny less and Memory Lane becomes a boutique."

Megan swallowed hard. It couldn't be done! But it must. "Agreed."

She slipped her fingers into his and with the first spark of contact his grip tightened. "Actually, it'll be interesting watching you try to turn this business around."

Watching me squirm, you mean. She tried to wriggle her hand loose, but his grip was like a vise. Minutely he was easing her toward him, and she shut her eyes as his sweet, hot breath burned against her cheeks.

For a moment she might have been back in the French Quarter with the man she loved. But *this* man was her enemy...

When his lips were only a heartbeat away she pulled back. "Perhaps I didn't make myself clear. I am *not* part of the deal!"

Kathleen O'Brien, an American author from sunny Florida, started out as a newspaper feature writer and television critic but happily traded that job in for marriage to an upwardly mobile journalist, motherhood and the opportunity to work on a novel. She finds romance writing especially satisfying, as it allows her to look for—and find—all the good things in life. Her Harlequin Presents novel, *White Midnight*, won the 1989 Maggie award for short contemporary romance.

Books by Kathleen O'Brien

HARLEQUIN PRESENTS
1011—SUNSWEPT SUMMER
1189—WHITE MIDNIGHT

KATHLEEN O'BRIEN

dreams on fire

Harlequin Books

TORONTO • NEW YORK • LONDON
AMSTERDAM • PARIS • SYDNEY • HAMBURG
STOCKHOLM • ATHENS • TOKYO • MILAN

To my mother, Lucy Fulghum O'Brien,
who is so often an inspiration

Harlequin Presents first edition May 1990
ISBN 0-373-11267-X

CHAPTER ONE

MEGAN FARRELL stroked her thumbs along the soft spines of one of the books longingly, fighting the rush of acquisitive desire that swept through her. Oh, how she wanted to say yes! She shut her wide gray eyes, drinking in the pungent odor of fine leather. A complete set of Shakespeare's plays from the early 1800s...it was the find of a lifetime.

Such a beautiful set, the pages pliable under her exploring fingers and still creamy white below their cool gold edges. Even the leather binding was uncracked. Someone had loved these books. *She* would love these books.

Wiping back the dark curl that had tumbled onto her brow, she fought an intense battle with her common sense. She couldn't afford them. Even now an alarmingly tall stack of stamped envelopes sat on her desk, mutely reproachful at being still-unmailed—bills, bills and more bills. Here in the French Quarter, rent alone could break the store if she weren't careful.

Stealing a glance at the man across the desk, Megan quickly calculated how much she could afford to offer for the set. Her heart sank. So little left after the envelopes had been dropped in the mailbox. It would be an insult—and yet she could tell in the defeated set of his shoulders that he would probably accept any offer.

Ruefully she eased her hand away from the books. She just couldn't take advantage of his desperation. Even if she had been tempted to, it would have been like breaking faith with Natalie's memory. "We're a couple of softies, Meggie," Natalie had said, with an ironic but not unsatisfied sigh. "Naive, my husband called it, and he may have been right. Ideals won't pay the rent."

Megan clenched her jaw as she pictured Natalie's frail figure as she had last seen it, looking so lost in the four-poster bed. Natalie's once-acerbic tones had been muted as she'd tried to explain her new will, the one that would always guarantee a job for Megan at Memory Lane, but which would leave the store itself to the son Natalie hadn't seen for twenty years, Ashton Hartford Chadbourne III.

Suddenly the wistfulness vanished, and Megan compressed her full lips. That name alone was enough to banish sentimental tears. Natalie had warned her that her son would be a tough taskmaster. "He was only ten when I left New York," Natalie had said grimly. "But he was already his father's son. Money, that's all they care about. I never had to worry about other women...the Chadbournes have never loved anything but themselves and their money."

Natalie had been so right. For the past six months all Megan's decisions down here in New Orleans had been thoroughly scrutinized. Already she had been required to send her bookkeeping and her inventories, her rental agreements, her insurance policies, her tax statements, everything, to the Chadbourne & Kelly offices in New York. She knew how it must look to them—the high expenses and the low profits, the minimum wages and the maximum reinvestment in merchandise. The careful lawyers' words had subtly revealed their dissatisfaction.

Megan's chest constricted with annoyance. No wonder Natalie had found being married to the elder Chadbourne unendurable. The odious Ashton Hartford III undoubtedly couldn't fathom the concept of working for the love of the work. But now it was up to Megan to prove that Natalie's little business could survive. Consequently her New Year's resolution would be to keep a firmer eye on the bottom line.

But, oh, these wonderful books! She glanced up at the banjo clock, which hung on the paneled wall between the bookcases. Six more hours before the New Year rang in officially. . . .

She shook the temptation away with a toss of her dark curls. No fudging.

Knitting her brows above a rueful smile, she dragged her gaze from the books.

"They're divine," she admitted. "But I can't pay you what they're worth." She dropped her hand to the top book and sighed. "I'm sorry."

The man frowned. "Well, what could you offer? I wouldn't be selling them if I didn't really need to."

"I know," she sighed again. "I know." She rustled through her card file, biting her lower lip. Finally she found the card she sought and held it out with a smile. "This is the address of another rare-book store here in New Orleans. I'm not sure they're open today, because of the holiday, but it might be worth waiting. They could pay you what the books are worth."

The man squinted at the card. "Well, thanks," he said dubiously. "I appreciate that. I really do." He slid the card into his pocket and began laying the books back into his box. Megan watched miserably as *Midsummer Night's Dream*, *Hamlet* and finally *Romeo and Juliet* disappeared from her envious view. At times like these she almost understood the money lust that drove some people. Almost.

But not enough to do this nice man out of his fair profit. "Happy New Year," she called as the door fell shut behind him, and then forced her attention to the other customers, who, although it was closing time, were still browsing, reluctant perhaps to go out into the darkening winter evening.

"Let me know if I can help you with anything," she told the room collectively and turned back to the stack of postcards she had been pricing. Let them browse a little longer. She wasn't in any hurry to leave. She hadn't even made up her mind where she was going....

Her mind skittered away from the dilemma, unable to confront it yet. Instead she stretched her back against the chair, trying to relax, and surveyed the funny little store she loved so dearly. Particularly tonight it was a haven to her, and she felt safe within its walls.

From the first day she had seen Memory Lane, she had felt at home here. It was more like someone's living room than a store. Along the back wall cherry bookcases were lined with the maroons and golds of rich old classics. In the center of the room, nestled beside leather armchairs, small lacquered ships' boxes overflowed with brilliantly colored antique maps and turn-of-the-century magazines. A mahogany refectory table along the front wall was loaded with albums of old postcards—Tuck and Winsch and Gibson beauties filled one box, historical scenes of New Orleans another, flocked and glittered greeting cards another, and . . . well, it took days to discover all that Memory Lane contained.

And here, that day five years ago, at this same rosewood desk, Natalie Chadbourne had sat. At sixty years old her bright hazel eyes were full of intelligence as she quizzed her eager new employee, the then eighteen-year-old Megan Farrell. Oh, Natalie, she asked the face in her memory silently. Why did you have to leave Memory Lane to your son? God only knows what he'll do with it now...

Megan sighed as she flipped over another postcard and scribbled the price code on it. She missed Natalie so much. Not just because she needed advice about how much to pay for old *National Geographics* or how to tell whether an autograph was authentic. No. Today she missed Natalie's hard-earned wisdom about life itself. Natalie would know what she should do about tonight.

The banjo clock chimed the half hour, and still she was loath to ask the customers to leave. They were her buffer, her safety net. When they left she would be alone with the decision.

Through the windows she could see the first sparkling shards of rain, and she knew without a doubt that they were falling on Tony's broad shoulders as he waited, perhaps not so patiently tonight, for her to join him. She shivered as the rain intensified, slashing at the windows as though attacking her cocoon, forcing her to make a decision.

She let the postcard fall to the desk and rubbed her eyebrows numbly. It was almost frightening that Tony had come to mean so much to her in such a short time. Was it really only a week ago that she'd met him? She hadn't been looking for romance. It had been just a lonely Christmas Eve, the first since Natalie's death. Just a long, impromptu walk through the teeming French Quarter, because Natalie's big house in front of Megan's little carriage house had been too silent. The cold mist had chased her under the café awnings where he sat, alone, too, studying an empty coffee cup.

He had offered her the other chair, and casually they had begun to talk. And talk, and talk. For hours, about everything. About jazz and computers and Creole food, dogs and mountains and Colorized movies. And they had come back, as though by unspoken agreement, night after night, to walk under the lacy canopy of winter clouds.

Remembered pleasure rippled through her. It had been wonderful. More than wonderful. It had been transforming, like being someone else, not cautious Megan Farrell at all. She knew nothing about him, except his name, Tony Ford, and she didn't want to know more. For this one miraculous week it had been enough to know that he had a wide, slow smile, hair the color of polished mahogany that darkened to jet when the mist kissed it, and those eyes of hunter green. Enough to know that they thought alike on so many trivial subjects. Enough to know that last night, when he'd taken her in his arms, her body had tucked itself into his as though they had been matching pieces of a puzzle....

"Your mail, milady."

Startled, she frowned at the outstretched palm.

"What?" She followed the crisp blue sleeve up to its owner's handsome face. "Oh, Harry. Thanks." She took the mustard-colored envelope from him without pleasure. The lawyers for Chadbourne & Kelly again. She'd had enough of these missives in the past six months to last her a lifetime.

Harry tsked as, without being invited, he settled himself in the armchair. "Such enthusiasm. Aren't you afraid it'll go to my head?"

She looked at the head in question. Its cap of silky blond hair glistened under the chandelier, and the light blue eyes smiled lazily. He'd caused quite a sensation when he opened his jewelry store on their block, and he knew it.

"Just trying to distinguish myself from the adoring throng," she said with a chuckle as she ran her ivory letter opener through the edge of the envelope.

She was expecting another official request for information, but the red, white and blue rectangle of an airline ticket fell onto the table. She frowned at it, surprised.

"What's this?" Harry leaned over and scooped it up. "A ticket?" He flipped it open. "To New York? You have friends in New York?"

Megan shook her head blankly and unfolded the accompanying letter. As she read, her eyes narrowed with every word. Typical arrogance. Mr. Chadbourne had advised . . . Mr. Chadbourne would like . . . The message was clear. She was being summoned to New York, where Mr. Chadbourne would meet her to discuss the future of Memory Lane.

Harry reached out for the paper. "Have you been invited somewhere?"

"Invited?" She laughed, a short bark of irritation, and dropped the offending letter onto the desktop. "Like people were *invited* to the Tower of London. It's more like a command performance. Ticket and hotel reservations provided, without so much as a word to me. First-class, round-trip. Prepaid." She crumpled the envelope angrily and dumped it into the brass can at her feet. "Even the seat has been preassigned."

The blood beat high in her temples, and she drummed the desktop with the letter opener. How dare he? The ticket was for January 2, the day after tomorrow. How did he know she didn't have plans? And what made him think she could staff Memory Lane on such short notice? Besides, she couldn't afford to be gone now. The months between Thanksgiving and Mardi Gras in February were Memory Lane's best, and she needed every sale she could squeeze out of this season.

But even as she hotly ran through her list of grievances, she knew she wasn't being honest. She squeezed the opener hard, its cutting edge pressing against her palm. Chadbourne's arrogance annoyed her, of course, but the real reason she didn't want to go to New York was much more personal. It was simply that New York was so far from the little café in the French Quarter, so far away from Tony, who was still waiting.

Dropping the ivory shaft, she stopped herself short. She hadn't even decided to meet Tony tonight. Hadn't she been telling herself all day that she shouldn't, that Tony of the green eyes and mellow voice was dangerous, someone who might make her forget other resolutions she'd made?

Last night his hands against her skin had been like a lit match being held against an old piece of paper. She had felt herself catching fire, disappearing almost without resistance into a white-hot flame. If she went into those arms again, there would be nothing left of her firm resolve but ashes and smoke. She shuddered. She might be safer three thousand miles away, high in a Manhattan tower.

"Whoa, there!" Harry looked quizzical, and she realized he interpreted her panicked flush as anger. "A free trip to New York doesn't sound that bad to me. What're you getting all hot and bothered for?"

"Sorry," she said, running her fingers over the high arch of her brows. This wasn't any of Harry's business, really. "I'm not feeling up to a trip right now, I guess."

"Well, can't you just call them and tell them you can't make it?" His irrepressible curiosity, she realized, wouldn't let him drop it. "Just tell them you're sick or something?"

She shook her head, thinking of the arrogance that asserted itself, even through the legalese. She imagined that it would be very difficult to tell Mr. Chadbourne no.

She picked up her purse and stuffed the ticket in it. Blast it. She *really* didn't want to go. How was she going to be polite to this man she despised, this man who worshipped money and would never understand Memory Lane? She jerked the zipper shut angrily.

"I don't think His Highness would like that," she said with a grim smile.

"His Highness? Is that what you call—what's his name?"

"Ashton. Ashton Hartford Chadbourne III, Esquire."

He grinned. "Sure sounds like royalty. What a name! All those last names strung together. Mom's maiden name or what?"

"Beats me," she mumbled. "It's an absurd name. Pompous. Like the man."

"Oh, I don't know," he mused. "He probably has some chummy nickname—left over from his Yale days. Like Biff. Or Bash. Or Buck."

"Close enough," she said, smiling in spite of her annoyance. "They call him Ford. You know, for Hartford?"

"Ahhh." He leaned back in the chair and watched Megan out of the corners of his blue eyes. "So what's really wrong with this Ford fellow? How come you look like you smell something bad whenever you talk about him? You can't stand his guts, can you?"

She laughed shortly. "Right."

"But you've never even met him, have you? That doesn't seem exactly fair." He snorted. "Besides, I've noticed girls never hate a rich guy unless they absolutely have to. Like if he opens fire on your house with a machine gun or something."

"Let's just say I know his type." She put her hand on the desk, ready to stand. The customers had finally drifted out, and it was time to lock the door. "He's spoiled, superficial, self-indulgent, self-important, self-centered—and every other 'self' word you can think of."

"Oh, poor devil." Harry laughed and stood up, too. "And he actually *wants* to get together with a spitfire like you?" She didn't return his grin, and, still chuckling, he changed the subject. "Well, I didn't come here to get a lecture on the evils of the Chadbourne family anyway. I came to see if you're going to join us at the hotel."

Her focus shifted to the windows behind Harry's head, where the rain was still falling heavily. "I don't know— I've got a lot of merchandise to price...." She still wasn't ready to make a decision. How could heart and mind be at such a stalemate? Picking up a scarf, she turned to the Empire mirror behind the desk and laid the silk over her curls.

Smoothly Harry's face joined hers in the mirror. "Oh, come on, Megan. You've got to. The whole street is going to be there. It's New Year's Eve." He put his hands on her shoulders. "It would be good for you. You look tense," he added, his voice low. "A little champagne. A little night music..."

She met his eyes calmly. How he would have hated to know that not one flutter passed through her as his hands stroked the curve of her shoulders.

She tried to smile. He wasn't a bad guy, really. Just boring. And he couldn't know that pretty boys had never been her weakness. She hadn't even known until last night that she *had* a weakness. But she did. She did.... Her heart tripped slightly, and her breath caught.

Last night, with one shattering kiss, with one endless moment of hard hands against soft skin, she had discovered that, like all steely things, she could be as weak as rubber when raised to the right temperature. Yes, she had a weakness all right—for green eyes and mellow laughter and hard lips.

She cast suddenly frantic eyes toward her reflection. Just thinking about Tony had given her that look, the look that had, since she was a teenager, made men smile her way, the look that was making Harry squeeze her shoulders even tighter now.

For a moment she tried to analyze its source impartially. It wasn't beauty, exactly. Maybe it had something to do with her coloring. Though she wore no makeup, her black, arched brows and thick curl of lashes had a theatrical flair, and a nervous heat had flushed her high cheekbones until they matched the crimson of her full, red lips. Or maybe it was just that her thoughts showed in her eyes. The blue of her shirt was reflected in their gray pools, and they were softly inviting.

She stared helplessly at the vivid creature in the mirror, and again she tried to push thoughts of Tony from her mind. She didn't want to look—or feel—this way. For a miserable moment she might have been little Meggie again, the orphaned convent-school boarder whose flamboyant looks had so distressed the nuns.

Sister Margarite's pinched voice echoed back through the years. "We'll have trouble with that one," the black-clad figure had whispered to her sisters as Meggie walked by in her uniform, that plain blue jumper that mysteriously hung so seductively on her. "It's in her blood."

The other nuns had nodded. "Blood will show."

Blood will show. For months the words had followed little Meggie everywhere she went, terrorizing her with murky implications of disaster. And then, after years of silence, she had heard the words again last night, when Tony had held her, when her body had seemed to glow under his caress with a strange and wonderful light. For a moment it had seemed so right—more like Destiny than dalliance, more like Fate than flirtation. *Love*, her heart had whispered. *I love this man.*

But then the words had raced back at her. Impossible, they'd said. In one week? *Love?* No. Lust, they had jeered. Blood will show.

"Okay," she said suddenly. Surprised, Harry lifted his lips from their descent toward her shoulder.

"Okay?"

"Yes." She tied the scarf tightly, too tightly, under her chin. "I'll come. But don't pick me up. I'll join you there later, and I don't know how long I can stay. I do have work to do—especially now that I have to take this wretched trip."

Harry was grinning. "Sure. Anything. This is great. Great."

Megan nodded absently and opened the shop door. Harry ran out first, waving as he sprang into his waiting car. But she lingered, twisting the key slowly in the lock. The cold rain fell on her lips, and for a minute her resolve faltered. Tony's kiss had tasted like rain. But kisses would never have been enough. . . .

Her small heels clattering on the wet pavement, she rushed toward her car. It was over. Once again common sense had won. She didn't own the lovely Shakespeare volumes, and she wouldn't taste the clean wet kisses from

Tony's hard mouth.... But she wouldn't have to pay the price for those things, either. They cost too much.

THREE HOURS LATER she peered into her champagne, frowning at the watery reflection of dark hair and smoky eyes that floated there. Coming to the party had been a mistake. She should have stayed home with the late show, a glass of milk, a boring book.

Her hand tightened around the cold glass as the violins moaned under the bows' strokes, and, whisking the drink to her lips, she gulped and swallowed. She shut her eyes as the champagne slid down her throat, but the edgy feeling didn't go away.

Tilting the glass, she swirled the golden liquid around restlessly, and then pressed her hand over the rim. Bubbles broke from the base of the goblet and swam upward to burst against her palm. Damn—even that felt erotic. She let the glass thud back into place on the white cloth. Yes, she should have stayed home, locked in her room if necessary, until this obsession went away.

"Hi, there." A light hand tapped Megan on the head, rousing her. "Hmm. That's funny. You don't *look* like a coward."

Megan tilted her head and met the smiling brown eyes of her best friend, Becky Lawton.

"Me?" She pulled out the chair beside her, and Becky plopped herself down emphatically.

"Yes, you, Megan Farrell. I said you don't *look* like a coward." She took a swig of Megan's drink. "But you are."

Megan smiled at the emphasis in Becky's words. She was talking about a man—Becky was always talking about a man. Yet such fervor was out of sync with her usual lazy cynicism.

Becky, the only daughter of a New Orleans Brahmin, was a master of the romance game, flirting with a new man every few months, instinctively gauging how fast she could race without losing control. Megan enjoyed watching Becky's machinations, which often raised well-plucked new Orleans eyebrows, but she knew better than to play the game herself. Though she was technically as innocent as a child, she knew that, once awakened, her sensuality would be demanding, absolute. Should she ever give herself—any of herself—to a man, it would be everything, and it would be forever.

With an effort she brought herself back to the question. "Coward? Do you mean because of Harry?"

Becky waved mention of Harry aside with one airy hand. "Lord, no. Though he did sound pretty funny when he called to say you were coming. I swear his voice was squeaking."

Giving a knowing chuckle that would have shocked her strict parents, Becky pointed a pink fingernail at Megan. "No, ma'am. You know what I'm talking about. I'm talking about Mr. Right, who's out there, waiting in this wretched rain for you."

"Ahhh...." Stalling, Megan took another sip of champagne. "I decided not to go to him tonight."

Becky poked the table. "*You* are crazy. You're not really going to spend New Year's Eve with Hands-on Harry when you could be with Mr. Right, are you?"

Megan ran a hand through her curls, frustrated, and her rushed fingers caught on a snarl. She pulled at it roughly, wincing at the sting of torn hair. "Stop calling him that. It's ridiculous."

"Is it?" Becky leaned back in her chair and surveyed the room lazily. "Listen. I don't know how you did it in a city like this, but you've found yourself an honest-to-god romance. You can't let him get away. You told me yourself that it was special. That *he* was special."

"But that was before..."

Becky clicked her tongue, pursing pink lips. "Yeah, I know. That was before he got you in his arms. Well, for pity's sake, Megan—he was supposed to! You've been meeting him every night—you've both been drawn back to that spot like flies to honey. He *had* to kiss you! Lord, honey, you're crazy about each other. What are you so scared of?"

Megan glanced at the dance floor, where she had last seen Harry. Harry was safe. If romance was sweet, like exotic pastries, then Harry was cottage cheese. Perfect for a lady on a diet. No threat to peace of mind or battered willpower.

"I'm not scared," she said firmly. "I'm simply being prudent. I've only known him a week. I know almost nothing about him."

"So ask him his life history—if it's all that important. Though frankly I think it's more romantic this way."

Megan smiled. "You would."

"And so would you!" Becky's smile grew a whisper smaller—it was as close as she ever came to a serious expression. "Now listen here. You need to get out of here *now* and take a fast cab to the French Quarter. Sometimes you've got to risk a little bit. You're not one of those nuns you grew up with, you know. And unless I'm a pretty bad judge of character, which I am not, you're not fixing to become one."

Megan shifted uneasily. She had wrestled with the demon of her heritage for so long now that she hardly knew how to abandon the fight. But the thought was tempting, so tempting.

Her head spun, and she pushed aside the champagne, as though it were responsible for her confusion. She glanced around the room, searching for distraction, but there was no help here. In a shadowed corner a young man kissed the pink-tipped fingers of his partner, and, sighing, the woman clasped his hand to her cheek. Megan slammed her eyes shut, but it was too late. Her midsection twisted at the sight, and a sensation of longing for Tony shot from her knees to her own fingertips.

She held her breath, fighting the feeling. Rubbish! What all these people were experiencing—what she herself had been feeling all week—was just a delusion. A dangerous delusion.

With Harry, of course, there would be absolutely no delusions. As though her confusion had summoned him, he suddenly stood before her. "Dance, beautiful?"

Like a programmed robot she stood up to accept.

Becky tugged at her dress. "Hey—think it over, at least."

"I will," Megan agreed numbly. "I'll think about it."

Becky sighed, clearly frustrated, but she dropped her arm, and Megan swung onto the floor with Harry.

As it turned out, no thinking was required. She was dancing mechanically, her body on automatic pilot, when a hand tapped Harry's shoulder and he swiveled, looking annoyed.

"May I cut in?"

CHAPTER TWO

IT WASN'T a request. Though couched in polite terms, it was clearly a dismissal. Harry hesitated, as though prepared to refuse, but Tony's dark green eyes were locked onto Megan's face, and he didn't even acknowledge Harry's presence.

Megan dimly sensed Harry's indignation, half heard his grumble as he relinquished her, but it was as unimportant as static on an otherwise glorious recording. The only reality was the crescendo of pleasure that had burst within her breast.

She stared at Tony, unable to speak as the crescendo built to an unbearable pressure. Though each of his features had been in the fore of her memory every minute since she met him, a twinge of surprise pricked her—he looked different tonight.

Perhaps it was just that he was more formally dressed—all week he had worn jeans, and the fine wool of his gray suit now seemed too fragile to contain his broad shoulders and long, muscular thighs. Or that his thick, dark hair was subdued, combed neatly, no longer tousled by the night wind. Or perhaps the chandelier was picking out more gleaming auburn highlights from the mahogany than the winter moon ever had.

But no, it was more than that. His face, lean and taut, with a dramatic hollow that ran from cheekbone to lip in a deep, long line, was just a breath harder, the power of its strong bones more in evidence. His black, winged brows were pulled together slightly, furrowing the high, tanned forehead. His straight nose was always dominant, matching his square jaw and firm, cleft chin, but tonight the nostrils were more intensely flared. He didn't look angry, exactly, but he looked masterful, like a man who knew what he wanted and intended to get it. Witness how easily he had dismissed Harry.

Anxiety flicked at her, as brief and disturbing as the flash of a snake's tongue. She hadn't ever seen this side of him, this raw force. It reminded her of something...but what? She licked her lips and brought her gaze back up to his.

And then anxiety melted away. Whatever else was different, his eyes were the same. Those gorgeous deep green eyes, with their thick sweep of dark lashes, were warm and uptilted, as a slow smile spread across his full lips. She smiled back, her heart thumping.

"Trying to remember who I am?" he asked, a low laugh in his deep voice. But she could tell he was only teasing. He'd accepted her silent scrutiny confidently, obviously recognizing it for the incoherent mixture of pleasure and shock that it was.

As if she could ever forget him! If after fifty years of absence he came to her, she would know him instantly. She would know him in the black longing of memory, just as she knew him now in the dazzled blindness of first love.

"No," she murmured unnecessarily. "I guess I'm just surprised to see you... How did you find me?"

"It wasn't hard," he said, one side of his wide mouth pulling up in the hint of a grin. "Why? Do you wish I hadn't?"

"Oh, no!" The words raced to escape her lips. "I'm so glad."

"Then come here, Meggie," he said, tugging her into his arms. "Dance with me."

She knew she should ask more questions, but her blood had slowed to a languid torpor, and the questions didn't seem important enough to bother. She let her head fall to his shoulder and shut her eyes, wanting only to feel his hard hands and smell the clean, damp odor of his skin.

Now that he was here, her doubts were evaporating, like puddles in the sun. As improbable as it seemed, this *was* real. It was important. How could she have let the echoes of Sister Margarite's tight voice define it otherwise? Love, this kind of love, was not measured in minutes clocked, in pleasantries exchanged, in facts compiled. It was bigger and darker, brighter and more beautiful, than anything she had ever seen before. And she knew in a flash as bright as a strobe against the night, it was inevitable.

"Happy?"

She was so close to him she could feel the vibrations in his chest as he spoke. "Yes," she answered, pressing even closer.

"So am I." His voice held a small note of surprise, as though he had not expected to be.

She wondered briefly why that should be so. He seemed to her to be a man accustomed to having whatever he wanted. Surely he was accustomed to being happy. Or was it that he, too, was surprised to feel so strongly about someone he had known such a short time? She sighed heavily, relaxing further into his strong arms. Oh, there was so much to learn about him.

"It'll be midnight soon," she said. "The place will be a madhouse then."

He eased her away from him a little and gazed down at her with eyes that were suddenly hot and as green as melted emeralds. "Do you want to leave?"

Her cheeks grew warm under his gaze, as though the fire behind his eyes were burning her. He read so easily between her words. She *did* want to leave. She resented the people who crowded around them, making real intimacy impossible.

"Yes," she murmured, meeting his gaze bravely, though she knew her feelings could be seen in the smoky depths of her eyes. "We could go to my house. It's not far, and it's quiet."

His eyes narrowed. "What about him?"

"Who?" Puzzled at first, she couldn't imagine what he meant. Then she remembered. Poor Harry—so completely forgotten so quickly. "I didn't come with Harry," she said. "He's just a friend. I came alone."

She looked toward the tables where her friends and fellow shopkeepers had gathered. Harry sat next to Becky, flirting conspicuously with her. Becky looked up, catching Megan's eye, and winked, raising her fist in jubilant approval.

A low chuckle above Megan's ear proved that Tony had seen, too, and without another word he took her hand and led her across the floor. There was no time for goodbyes or explanations. She tossed Becky a brief wave as they moved toward the doors, the music receding behind them like the disappearing strains of a dream. And then they were outside, with the silver rain slicing the air.

"My car's just over there," she said, pointing. Though they had lingered many a night in rain like this, tonight she was compelled to rush.

"I've got a car, too," he said. "I'll follow you."

Surprised, she followed his eyes. Funny, she had never thought of his having a car. Every night he had just always been there, waiting for her at the café. And when he'd seen her to her car, she had always driven off, watching his disappearing figure in her rearview mirror. But of course, he had to have a car. She didn't know where he lived, but chances were great that he didn't live in the French Quarter, and he had to get here somehow.

But when she saw where his eyes had settled, she was even more shocked. Off to the side, blithely slipped into a No Parking slot, a sleek black Ferrari glistened in the rain. From where they stood, she could just see the license plate. It was a rental car. She squinted up at him, the rain pricking at her eyelids. She hadn't even known people could rent Ferraris.

It must have cost a fortune. And why did he have a rental car at all? A sudden, horrifying image of the classic traveling salesman reared its ugly head in her mind. Where *did* he live? Was she just a diversion—to help him pass the time as he was passing through town?

"Let's go." He put his strong hand on her back, and she began to walk, the light touch of his fingers somehow completely silencing her doubts.

They didn't speak again. His headlights shimmered just behind her as in silence she maneuvered the narrow length of Magazine Street and entered the hushed, manicured beauty of the Garden District, where she had lived for five years.

When she reached Natalie's old Victorian house, she pulled all the way around it and eased to a stop by the small carriage house in back. The Ferrari purred up behind her, and as she sat numbly watching, the engine died and the eyes of the headlights rolled shut.

She heard the tight click of his door, the soft slap of his feet across the wet driveway, and each sound was like a small stinging inside her.

He opened her car door. "Let's go," he said again, and she listened intently. Was there a hint of impatience in his voice?

She was glad he didn't express any surprise when she headed for the carriage house instead of the mansion behind them. He waited silently as she found her key. Her fingers were so clumsy she feared she couldn't manage the lock, but the key finally found its home, and she stood back to let him through.

"This is where you live?"

Nodding, she watched as his dark green eyes swept across the small living room, knowing his survey would be brief, for the room was tiny. No, it was *cozy*, she corrected herself quickly, surprising herself with the defensive note.

She straightened her back. Why should she feel defensive? It was a good room. But in spite of her mental pep talk, discomfort tightened her chest. Tonight Tony reminded her of something—and it made her slightly uncomfortable. Still braced against the door, she fingered the velvet leaves of an African violet and watched him.

As she marveled at his grace, his tapering back, the lush, springing hair above his elegant brow, gradually a new word insinuated itself into her thoughts. *Rich*. That was it—he was rich. His bearing was sleekly confident. His suit probably cost more than her entire wardrobe. And the Ferrari... Not just well-to-do. Rich. She swallowed hard. It wasn't her favorite word.

Her fingers tightened, snapping off a hapless leaf and releasing its pungent scent into the small room. How had she been so blind? Even without the Ferrari, she should have known. Should have seen that he looked exactly like those young social scions who occasionally ambled into Memory Lane to buy her most expensive old maps and first editions. They never haggled over prices—if they wanted something, they simply took it.

And was he like them? Oh, surely not! But still she watched, biting her lip, refusing to apologize for her humble home.

As he brought his eyes back to her, she felt her chin lift defiantly. This was who she was. If he couldn't accept it, if he judged people by their material possessions, it was better to find out now.

But to her immense relief his green eyes were smiling. "Nice," he said softly. "I like it."

Pleasure made her light-headed, and realizing that she had been holding her breath, she let her anxieties blow away with the exhaled air. Smiling foolishly and clutching her arms by the elbows, she simply said, "I'm glad."

She kept smiling, but her lips grew strained as her pulse started beating erratically, high in her neck. He looked so marvelous, his face dark above the deep, pointed white V of shirt beneath his suit. He wore no tie, just the luminous white shirt buttoned all the way up to his neck. The sight stirred her, arousing something wanton deep within. She wanted, madly, to reach out and pull open the buttons, revealing the taut mounds of his shoulders, the hard bands of his chest. She had to grip her elbows tightly to keep from giving in to the desire.

"Come here, Meggie."

She didn't move, though she felt a physical drag in her midsection, as though his voice were a magnet tugging at her from across the room. She gripped her elbows harder, as though to hold herself in place.

"Come here." His voice deepened, but she just shook her head slightly, unable to speak.

Narrowing his green eyes, he slowly crossed the few feet that stood between them. His hand stroked up the long column of her spine, dragging an electric current in its wake. Shivers exploded across her chest, but still she held her elbows.

"What's this?" His fingers strayed lightly over the goose bumps that sprinkled her cold shoulders. "You aren't afraid, are you?" His hands moved up, across the column of her neck. "You know I want you, Megan. I've wanted you since the first moment I saw you. But that's nothing to be afraid of, is it?"

"I'm not. I'm not afraid," she insisted raggedly, though it wasn't really true. "It's just that we've known each other such a short time. I don't even know if you're... if there's any reason why we shouldn't..."

He smiled, but it didn't lighten his smoldering green eyes. "Oh, no. There's no reason why we shouldn't." He pulled the gold filigreed clasp from her hair, letting the curls tumble around her shoulders. "In fact," he said, running his fingers through the thick blackness, "there's every reason why we should."

Her heart beat crazily, and she searched his face, as if she might find an explanation in the melting green eyes, the high forehead, the dark brows drawn slightly together. She couldn't understand herself. She had never been so weak with need before, though many men had tried to make her so. Was love, then, the most potent aphrodisiac of all? Was it love that filled her with this primitive need to fuse, to become, for a huge, reeling moment, one person, one body?

"You haven't changed your mind about me, have you?" His voice was smooth but masterful, like velvet-covered steel. She shut her eyes, letting that sound bury itself into the deepest part of her. His hands were still exploring the sensitive skin of her bare back, and the goose bumps crept into her hair.

She wondered briefly what he would do if she said yes, if she asked him to leave. But the thought was too brief to matter. His hard hands were sliding down under her dress, toward the small of her back, and already her legs were numb and shaking. All the blood in her body seemed to be racing to her midsection. She didn't want him to leave. His heart beat under her hands, and the slow, hardy rhythm was like a lifeline to which her heart clung.

"No," she said, eyes still shut. "I haven't changed my mind."

With a satisfied sound he reached his hands up, hot under her armpits as he lifted her off the floor and, gathering her possessively into his strong arms, carried her toward her bedroom.

And then he was kneeling over her, his hard thighs straddling hers and his hands roaming across her arms, her neck and finally her face.

"Look at me."

She opened her eyes, though her lids were so heavy it required an effort of will.

"Tell me that you want me, too." His eyes were glittering like green glass, and his hands were brushing her mouth, as though the hot fingers could pull from her lips the words he wanted to hear.

"I want you," she whispered. "I want you so much I can hardly breathe."

He didn't answer, but she heard a long, hollow intake of air through clenched teeth. His hands left her lips, twisting into her hair, pulling her head up off the pillow, up toward the hot demands of his mouth.

And then finally his lips were on hers, moving hot and hard, with an intensity of need that swept her up into a vortex as wild as the black needle of a tornado. The room careened around her and then seemed to disappear as she went willingly, clinging to his shoulders, asking only that he go with her into the darkness.

Last night's kiss had been as nothing compared to this, just the shivering of a branch in the wind. This was more. This was the complete uprooting, a brute force that left her jagged, exposed, all her firm ideas about herself torn asunder.

And it swept away completely the inhibitions in which she had been wrapped for so long. It was extraordinarily freeing, and her blood spun in her ears, as if she were free-falling through the night sky.

Quickly, with hands that no longer shook, she opened the buttons of his shining white shirt and buried her fingers in the dark hair of his chest. And as he slid open the zipper at the back of her dress, she explored the contours of his muscled torso, his tapered waist, his lean hips, with her own eager hands, glorying in the low, urgent moan her touch elicited.

He pulled the dress from her shoulders. She had worn nothing underneath the low-cut bodice, and her rounded breasts lay exposed, thrust toward him in innocent invitation.

The frantic pace slackened as he slowly drew solemn hands up across her arms, past the ridge of her collar bone, and finally, reverently, down to the deep rosy tips that brushed against his naked chest.

"Oh, Tony," she whispered, as his fingers traced the round curves. His touch was tantalizingly light, and she had to fight the need to reach up and press it closer. He knew so much more than she about these things. In spite of her drowning need, she knew he must set the pace.

Her breath was coming hard, and her breasts rose and fell in the inadequate ivory light from her bedside lamp, swelling to a gleaming prominence, then dipping back to a shadowed mystery. Finally his hands came away, and, dropping his head, he brushed his cheek across her breasts. The nipples tightened, as if instinctively aware of the maddening nearness of his lips, and a cry escaped her. From what cosmic memory did she know so well how it would feel for his hot, wet lips to close around them and pull them into the darkness of his mouth?

She shifted, need pulsing in her like the stab of a white-hot poker. Slowly he slipped further down, pulling the rustling silk dress as he went, until it was only a shimmering blue puddle at the foot of the bed and only the sheerest wisp of black lace hid her from his gleaming eyes.

She waited, willing her body to lie still, though her breasts felt swollen, as if the fragile pink skin were being stretched, and her hips felt a primitive restlessness, as though a drum beat somewhere and she must answer it. Her stomach tingled where the fabric lay against her, nerve endings on fire as they awaited the slow drag of lace across her skin that would finally set her free.

"You're a miracle," he whispered, stroking the tender skin of her inner thigh. She shuddered helplessly. "You're so passionate—and yet there is such an innocence about you."

With a groan he shifted his weight, and she felt the fierce straining of his own desire. She was not alone in this torment. Blindly she reached up toward his belt. "Tony..."

"No." He stilled her hands and pressed them back against the pillow, holding them palms up, his fingers locked around the wrists. "First you have to tell me—is this all right? Is it safe for you?"

At first she couldn't understand him. Did he mean morally? It was a little late for that, wasn't it? Or did he realize she had already fallen in love with him and was in danger of suffering a broken heart? Or did he mean . . .

Her breath froze in her throat as the truth crashed on her, as violently as if she had been struck by lightning. She pulled her hands away and covered her eyes, blinded by returning reality. He was right—she hadn't ever, not even once, given any thought to her safety. And of all people, she should have.

Oh, god! What a fool he must think her—what a fool she thought herself! And yet, though her mind understood that he had brought her to her senses just in time, still her body was wracked with the need he had created. For a brief, agonized moment, she wished she could lie, could say that she *had* protected herself, so that he would hold her again. In an instant, though, sanity returned, and, horrified that such a deception should even occur to her, she pulled away from him, reaching blindly for her discarded dress.

Sister Margarite had been right. She had spent years girding herself against this very thing, years vowing she would never end up like her mother. And here she was, ready to throw her vows away, ready to let her boiling blood lead her into a lifetime of misery. Blood, after all, will tell.

But how could she explain any of this to him? To him she might be just another naive kid, the kind of irresponsible young woman who could someday end up on his doorstep, whimpering and threatening, asking for sympathy, or money—or more. And in his case, there was obviously so much for him to lose. It might even have happened before. No wonder he had remembered to ask. Rich men didn't take such chances, not even when they were fiery with desire.

He had stood up now, too, and his breathing was harsh and deep as he stared at her from across the bed. The rumpled white coverlet between them might have been a raging, storm-white ocean, a distance they could never bridge. Averting her head to hide her glittering eyes, she fumbled with her zipper. Her fingers were clumsy, and it was difficult even to stand, for his caresses had left her strangely weak, her legs as unreliable as stalks of melting wax.

"What are you doing?" His voice was different, rasping, and she winced under the sound as if he had raked a file across her skin. How disgusted he must be!

"Obviously I'm getting dressed," she said and realized her voice, too, sounded harsh and strained. "I'm sorry," she added, ashamed of her sniping tone and working to control it. "This has all been a terrible mistake." It wasn't his fault. She had acted, from the first meeting at the café to the easy submission here tonight, as though such things came often and casually in her life. And then, as always, there were her looks, that trick of nature that had sculpted a wanton face to mask her cautious soul. What else could he have thought? "This was all very stupid of me."

"Yes, obviously it was."

The flat criticism, though entirely justified, went through her with a jagged stab, and she leaned against the wall. She had allowed herself to hope that he would understand. Wrapping her fingers around the cold scrolls of the brass headboard, she tried to fight back the scalding tears of humiliation that threatened to drown her eyes.

Why didn't he put on his shirt? She wanted desperately to be alone. She didn't know how much longer she could stand the dark judgment in his face, or the throbbing void inside her own body, without breaking down.

"I think you should go now," she whispered, pushing her tangled curls away from her damp brow. "I'm sorry."

But he still didn't lean down to retrieve his shirt. Instead, he took a deep, ragged breath and walked slowly around the foot of the bed. He took her shoulders in his hands, and she could feel the tension in them, making his fingers stiff.

She shook her head hurriedly, her face flaming. "No." The syllable sounded strangled, and his eyes darkened at the sound, his fingers gripping harder. "Don't you see— I just got carried away, Tony. I'm sorry. I shouldn't have—I can't."

"Don't do this, Megan." His voice was strained, harsh.

"Do what?"

"Act like a damned, idiotic virgin." He shook her shoulders. "We've come too far. It's too late to lie to me—or to yourself."

She couldn't risk looking at him, at the geometrically sculpted muscles of his chest and arms, at the hard, parted lips, the darkly burning eyes. It was too tempting, and she didn't trust her willpower. *Willpower*—the very word seemed to taunt her. Her flesh burned as she remembered how wantonly she had reached for him. She could almost see Sister Margarite smirking. And she could feel the shame.

"No," she repeated dully.

"But *why*?" He sounded angry now, and his hands were punishing against her bruised shoulders. "Dammit, Megan. *Why!*"

"I just can't . . ." Her voice was thick and she couldn't go on. "Please go. Please."

For a moment his grip was so tight on her that she wondered whether his anger and his desire would overcome him, but finally he dropped his hands and with a smothered oath turned away. For a paralyzed moment the room was silent, touched only by the distant rumble of frustrated thunder and faint flashes of tired lightning from the dying storm. Then in a rough gesture he whipped up his shirt and flung it across his shoulders, pulling the buttons harshly through their abused slits and jamming the shirttails under his belt.

He stood, fully dressed, and gazed at her. The light in the room was too dim for her to read his expression, but his rigid stance spoke volumes. She parted her lips, hoping to find words that would make sense, but nothing came.

From outside she heard the scattered gunshot of fireworks, the eerie, descending wail of Roman candles. Midnight. The moment at which the promise of a new year was fulfilled. She felt a black spurt of laughter pushing at the back of her tight throat. She had hoped for something so different.

The excited shouts of exuberant revelers echoed through the small room, and he stooped to pick up his discarded jacket. Holding it with a crooked forefinger over his broad shoulder, he moved toward the door, turning back only for an instant, to say in a deep voice filled with irony, "Happy New Year, Megan."

THE AIR WAS COLD, and she shifted on the bed, her unconscious mind registering the uncomfortable temperature. There was something else—a dull ache of unhappiness, vague and generalized, like the slow return of pain as an anesthetic wears off. And what was that sound? She burrowed deeper under her quilt.

But the sound wouldn't stop, and slowly she opened her eyes. Sun streamed in through the windows, laying pale yellow stripes against the lavender walls. New Year's Day had dawned cold and cloudless, and the telephone was ringing.

She jerked up, a formless, nameless hope ballooning in her chest. The violet-sprigged quilt fell away from her, and she crawled, bunching her sleep-wrinkled skirt up in one fist, across the bed to the telephone.

She picked it up quickly. "Hello?"

"Miss Farrell?"

Sinking back onto her heels, Megan acquiesced indifferently, not bothering to try to place the brisk, businesslike voice. It wasn't Tony. For a moment that piercing disappointment was all that mattered.

"This is Jim Brackett," the voice went on. "Ford Chadbourne's secretary. I'm calling from New York. I'm trying to reach Mr. Chadbourne."

Megan frowned and let her skirt fall to cover her bare feet. "I beg your pardon?"

The voice was patient. "I'm trying to find Mr. Chadbourne."

A quick sprinkle of goose bumps dotted her bare shoulders. It was suddenly so cold in her little empty room. "Why are you calling *here*? Isn't he in New York?"

"Why, no. No, he's been in New Orleans all week. Didn't you know that? He told me he'd been spending time with you." The voice grew confused, stumbling. "He gave me your number—yesterday. He said...he said if I couldn't get him at the hotel this morning, to try your place."

CHAPTER THREE

THIRTY-SIX HOURS later, Megan stood on the fortieth floor of the Chadbourne building and looked out at the jigsaw puzzle of rooftops that was New York. It was late. The sunset's hot, red rim was reflected in the glass walls of nearby buildings, seeming to set them on fire.

But here in the Chadbourne & Kelly offices everything was cool and efficient. Even through her numbed haze she felt an angry throb of satisfaction that Ford Chadbourne's world was just as soulless as she had imagined: a sterile, ultra-modern showplace, all angular art and smoke-and-silver furniture. Even the receptionist fit the stereotype—a striking redhead with a thousand-watt smile and a Muzak voice.

Oh, Ashton Hartford Chadbourne was slick, all right. Slick enough to run a multimillion-dollar company and slick enough to make a pretty fool out of her. Tony Ford indeed!

She dug her fingernails into her palms, forcing herself to stand calmly in case he should emerge and see her. *A fool.* It wasn't a role she was used to. Megan Farrell was always in control, at least on the surface. If more passionate emotions simmered uneasily beneath that veneer of restraint, she was the only one who knew it. She didn't want exotic, turbulent emotions. As an illegitimate child, she had seen first-hand the shame to which those things led you.

She had asked only one thing out of life—safety. She just wanted to work quietly at Memory Lane among the old, beautiful things and live quietly in New Orleans, harbored from life's more treacherous currents.

She grimaced now, remembering how Natalie had scolded her on the subject. "This isn't a cocoon, Megan. Sure, there's trouble out there, but if you don't go out and grab it by the tail, it's just going to come in here and get you."

And Natalie knew all about trouble. She had never confided to Megan exactly why she had left her husband, but Megan knew it must have been something unendurable, or she would never have left her son as well, no matter what. That Natalie had still loved her son, in spite of the long years of absence, was clear. She had left him Memory Lane, hadn't she?

Megan squeezed her eyes shut against the blazing, sinking sun and bowed her head. Well, Natalie's predictions certainly had come true. She thought she had hidden from fear, from heartbreak, from pain. And then, two nights ago, she had opened her door and invited it in.

Oh, how *could* she have missed that flippant twist of names? Ashton Hartford/Tony Ford. It was, she realized now, almost insultingly transparent. And the eyes, Natalie's beautiful green eyes—how had she failed to recognize them? Folding her arms tightly across her chest, she flicked the thoughts away impatiently. She had asked herself the same questions hundreds of times in the past miserable hours. It was stupid and defeating, like being stuck in a revolving door. There was no answer, no justification. She hadn't seen through the charade, that's all. She had been a fool.

"Can I get you a cup of coffee, Miss Farrell?" The redhead was at her elbow, efficient, solicitous. Without turning, Megan shook her head.

"No, thank you," she said coolly. She knew what the offer meant. Chadbourne was going to keep her waiting. Well, that was all right. She could take it. She raised her chin and stared straight into the sunset. She had come a long way since that sickening plummet into despair yesterday morning, when she had discovered that her wonderful Tony Ford had never really existed, that it had been Ford Chadbourne all along, playing games, the way rich boys do.

Her hands felt cold, and tucking them deeply into the soft wool of the suit she had borrowed from Becky, she breathed deeply again.

She was ready for him this time. Becky had a model's flat figure, so the borrowed suit was a little tight across the chest on Megan, but it was expensive, professional and a superconfident ruby red. She had highlighted her full lips with a matching shade of lipstick and shaded her gray eyes with a silvery blue shadow that made them look as hard and beautiful as gunmetal. She had raked her wild tangle of curls back tightly, forcing them into submission with that foamy white goo she ordinarily despised, and clipped it into a neat silver circlet.

She hoped he would be surprised. If he expected her to come crawling in here, sniveling and ashamed, he would certainly be disappointed. Megan Farrell crawled for no one, especially not for Ashton Hartford Chadbourne, who was only a liar and a fraud.

"Miss Farrell? Mr. Chadbourne will see you now." The redhead was ready with another solicitous smile and led the way to the huge double doors at the end of the hall.

Megan strode through them with the blind, determined courage of a queen entering the tumbril. Though she dimly sensed a quiet, nondescript presence in a far corner of the room, she fixed her eyes on Chadbourne—he looked absurdly tall as he stood behind his desk—and headed straight for him, her red lips parted in a slightly mocking smile and her hand outstretched.

"Mr. Chadbourne. How nice to see you again so soon. I can't tell you how sorry I am that you didn't have more fun while you were in New Orleans. Our winters are so wretchedly wet, you know. I trust you didn't have the bad luck to catch a cold."

It was a gratifying moment. Clearly, he *was* surprised. His hard hand was arrested in midair, and his green eyes squinted just a little, as though he couldn't believe what they were showing him. Good, she thought grimly. This round may just go to me, Mr. Chadbourne.

But almost immediately he recovered himself and smiled appreciatively at her bravado. The effect of that smile was devastating. She felt the now-familiar twist in the pit of her stomach, the clutch at her chest, the humiliating weakness in her knees. She took the hand he extended but let it go after the briefest touch and looked pointedly at the chair.

"May I sit down?"

For answer he inclined his head a crisp inch, a noncommittal movement indicating neither invitation nor rejection. He must have been learning these power games since he was at his father's knee, she thought grimly as she lowered herself onto the straight-backed chair. It had been strategically placed so that she had to stare into the sunset, which was now concentrated in one throbbing stripe of flame right behind his head.

She settled herself as comfortably as possible, carefully covering her knees with Becky's bright red skirt as she crossed them. Folding her hands neatly in her lap, she continued to smile into his green eyes, waiting for him to speak first. After all, he was the one who'd issued the summons.

"No, I was lucky, Megan. I may call you Megan?" He didn't pause for an answer, and she contented herself with lifting one arched brow sardonically. "I didn't suffer any ill effects at all. I think I got back to New York just in time."

"How fortunate," she said. "And all this?" She waved her hand languidly at the stacks of paper in his leather tray. "Your business didn't suffer, either, I trust? I know that's probably as important as your health to you—more important, perhaps." She smiled wickedly as his brows knitted slightly, furrowing his high brow. "Goodness, I was frankly surprised that you were willing to take a whole week off from all this. I thought all business moguls were workaholics. Can the Chadbourne & Kelly widgets actually be made without your physical presence?"

"We don't make 'widgets,'" he cut in, his voice clipped.

She leaned back in her chair. So she had been right. This was his Achilles heel. His business. His money. His power. Though she had known it would be so, still she felt a surge of disappointment. Why was her fantasy of Tony Ford so persistent, so hard to destroy? Finding the real man should be no surprise. And yet it hurt, and the bitterness drove her on.

"Don't you? I was sure I had heard somewhere that you did—make widgets, that is."

"No. We don't. We make more machinery parts than any other company in the world. There isn't a factory in America that could stay in business without us."

"Oh, I see." She widened her eyes and pursed her lips in a circle of surprise. "I stand corrected. You make *lots* of widgets."

She refused to drop her gaze under his glinting green stare, though her fingers hurt from grinding them against one another in her lap. She hadn't realized until the stab of pain drove through her how tense she was. It was stupid, really, to be so offensive. She might despise Ford Chadbourne, but he held her future and the future of Memory Lane in his hands, and she was crazy to antagonize him.

She raised her chin. If they were enemies, it was his fault, not hers. He was the one who had deceived her. He was the one who had made a game, a nasty little game, of love. He was the one who...

He was laughing.

"Ouch. Somehow I don't think we've impressed Megan at all, do you, Jim?" At the name, Megan turned her head, finally focusing on the other presence in the room, a thin young man who sat on the edge of his chair, a folder in his lap, and laughed somewhat nervously.

"I guess not, Mr. Chadbourne," he said, with a quick glance in Megan's direction. Clearly he was not accustomed to hearing such blasphemy. He looked to his boss again, who was still chuckling.

"Maybe we should give her the VIP tour." Ford leaned back in his leather chair, and the pulsing sunset seemed to encircle his head like a crown. "Would you like that, Megan? Lots of machines that rumble and roar. Lots of widgets."

She could hear the smile in his voice, the smile that had already, in one short week, grown so familiar to her, and she clutched her hands tighter, breathing quickly. Perhaps it was just as well that his face was in shadows. If she could see that wide, melting smile...

"I don't think that will be necessary." Clearing her throat, she made her voice tough. "Our business together concerns only Memory Lane, doesn't it? There are no widgets there."

"No profits, either." Ford summoned the other man, who leaped from his seat as though the quick flick of Ford's long finger had been a cattle prod. He must be a very tough boss, she concluded and, narrowing her eyes, watched as Jim—it must be Jim Brackett, Ford's secretary and her early morning caller—spread the contents of his folder across the huge desk.

She recognized the papers—the rental contract, the sales receipts, all the information she had sent the Chadbourne & Kelly lawyers about Memory Lane. Here in this enormous mahogany office they seemed even more paltry than ever. She swallowed hard, ready to defend herself.

"That's not really fair, is it?" She tried to sound reasonable. "Memory Lane did quite well last year, actually. I've worked there five years, and Natalie never failed to make a profit."

"You call this a profit?" He dashed his fingertips dismissively against the small stack of papers. The playful tone he had used earlier was gone, replaced by the sound of the harsh New York businessman who had no time for pleasantries, no time for sentimental little mom-and-pop stores and no time for her. "It's pathetic. Apparently Natalie was as big a failure at running a business as she was at everything else."

She gasped, pulling in air so fast it made her light-headed. This was his mother he was talking about. How could anyone, even Ford Chadbourne, be so cruel?

"That's a horrible thing to say about your own mother," she sputtered, aware that she was sounding like an outraged child. Her angry breath came so fast and deep that her breasts pressed dangerously at Becky's tight jacket. She could feel the buttons straining at their clasps. How easily he had punctured her facade of cool indifference! Her face felt steamy with indignation, and she knew her cheeks must be flaming. But she couldn't pretend she didn't care. She had loved Natalie dearly and had seen how hard Natalie had worked.

But Ford didn't even look up, still idly pushing the papers around on his desk. Clearly her hot indignation bored him. God, he was ruthless—just as his father must have been. Forcing her lungs to take air in slowly, she strove for a tone that would reflect the true disgust she felt.

"Your *mother*," she said, stressing the word coldly, "was a wonderful woman. Memory Lane is a wonderful store. She didn't *want* to make huge profits. Unlike you, Mr. Chadbourne, she understood that life's successes aren't always measured in dollars and cents." Finally Ford looked up, and she stared at him through narrowed eyes, curling her lips scornfully. "She might not have been a success in *your* terms, but she was an enormous success in my eyes. She was a success as a person."

"Really?" Ford stared back at her, his green eyes granite hard. "I wonder what you would have thought of her performance as wife and mother." His voice was hollow and emotionless, as though the issue were a matter of indifference to him.

The tone infuriated her, and she shot her answer back between clenched teeth. "And *I* wonder what I would have thought of your father's performance as husband—more importantly, *your* performance as son."

This time the horrified gasp sounded from the other side of the room, where Jim Brackett had retreated to his inconspicuous corner. Through her fury she felt a grim satisfaction at the realization that she must be one of very few people who would have dared to speak to Ford Chadbourne this way. Good. This was one scored for her side, for the gullible Megan Farrell who had kissed this ruthless man in the moonlight.

Ford was leaning back again, in the classic corporate posture of aloof confidence. "Your loyalty does you credit, Megan," he said coldly, "especially as you managed to persuade Natalie to protect you so well in her will."

Ever alert to his tone Megan caught the subtle innuendo and protested hotly. "I didn't persuade—"

He waved her protests away. "The point is you have been guaranteed a job at Memory Lane as long as it stays open."

Suddenly Megan saw where the conversation was leading. It was just as she had feared these long six months. He would close down her beloved little store, sell all the charming books and cards at auction. Or would he even bother? He'd probably just throw them out like the rubbish he believed them to be. Her heart tightened painfully. Oh, no. Oh, please, no. But she refused to beg. She wrapped her pride around herself and lifted a calm face to his.

"Yes. That's right. She knew I'd grown to love the store, and she believed I was capable of running it."

He drummed his fingers restlessly on the desktop. "But are you, Megan? Your books indicate a twenty percent drop in sales in the six months since Natalie died, the exact period that you've been in charge."

"It has been a difficult time," she said slowly, stung by the truth of his accusations. "When Natalie died, it was so hard to—"

"That's no excuse," he broke in impatiently. "Memory Lane obviously has always survived by the skin of its teeth. But another six months like that and it would be bankrupt. There's no room for sentiment in business."

She hated the heartless tone in which he dismissed her pain. Had he felt nothing himself when his mother died? Had the Chadbourne & Kelly widgets just kept right on rolling from their high-tech factories, with not a heartbeat's stumble? She pressed her lips together hard to keep them from trembling. How could she ever have believed he was someone she could love?

"No sentiment at all," she repeated dully. "That is undoubtedly a tenet you can live by with no difficulty."

His eyes were stormy, but his response was interrupted by a loud fussing at the door. As the three in the room watched curiously, the sound of raised voices was followed by the emphatic click of the handle, and the big door swung open.

Megan caught her breath. The two women who breezed in were perhaps the most beautiful creatures she had ever seen. At first glance they could have been twins—both gleaming ash blondes, with flawless alabaster skin and nearly identical, poised, trim figures under expensive peaches-and-cream suits.

As they moved forward, though, she observed the subtle differences that proved them to be not twins but mother and daughter. The woman who led the way had

achieved her smooth skin surgically it seemed, her ash-
blond hair chemically. A hardness marred the expression in her eyes, a hardness not evident in her daughter's
sweet pale blue ones. Not yet, anyway, Megan thought,
and then regretted her easy criticism when she met the
endearing difference of the younger woman's smile.

"Ford," the older woman was saying as she swept
across the Turkish carpet in a cloud of expensive perfume. "Ford, what a jewel your new girl is. We practically had to threaten the poor thing to get past her. She
makes a wonderful keeper of the gate. You must explain
to her, though, that Krista and I don't exactly constitute
an 'interruption.'"

Ford had risen politely and gave the older woman a
perfunctory kiss on the cheek. "Indeed you don't, Felicia. But Linda's *very* new. And I did tell her not to let
anyone in."

The younger girl came closer to accept her own kiss,
which was somehow both sweeter and more protective
than the one Ford had given her mother.

She smiled up at him with limpid blue eyes. "I am so
sorry, Ford, really, to bother you. I hate to interrupt your
meeting. It's just that mother..."

Ford reached out and nudged her cheek with the back
of his hand. Megan's own cheek flamed as she watched,
and she prayed he wouldn't see. She knew all too well
how that strong hand would feel. But she would forget.
She clenched her teeth and fought back the crazy desire
that curled disagreeably in her stomach. She would forget.

"Hey, it's okay, Kris. Don't worry so much." Ford's
voice, gentle and soothing, was so much like the voice
Megan remembered from the evenings in the French
Quarter that tears burned behind her eyes. How could she

have been such a fool as to believe his interest in her had ever been serious?

It was a story as old as time—certainly as old as her own disgraceful birth. She had been a fling—a spot of fun to liven up a dull week in a rainy Southern backwater. She was just a pretty little nobody with red lips and a dance-hall body and no one to defend her.

Only a woman like this Krista, this vision of well-bred, muted glamor, whose mother stood dragonlike behind her to guard her virtue and her future, would be considered a worthy partner for Ashton Hartford Chadbourne III.

"Felicia, Krista—I'd like you to meet Megan Farrell." At the sound of the inevitable introductions, Megan dragged her thoughts away from their mournful musings and tried to smile. She immediately regretted the too-tight, borrowed, red suit. She licked nervously at the lipstick she had applied so defiantly this morning, wishing it were less red.

"Megan worked for Natalie at her store in New Orleans," Ford continued in his deep tones. "Natalie mentioned her in her will, you'll remember. We were just working out some of the details. Megan, this is Felicia Kelly and her daughter, Krista. Since her husband, Patrick, died some years ago, Felicia has been the 'Kelly' of Chadbourne & Kelly."

Kelly. Megan squinted as though warding off a physical blow. Patrick Kelly. Apparently she forgot to breathe, for the room blurred and began to swirl wildly around her. The blond women smiling in front of her faded in and out of focus for what seemed like an aeon, and then Megan felt herself smiling and shaking their hands, accepting the cool reluctance of Felicia's fingers and then the warmer, lingering touch of Krista's clasp.

"Hello," she heard herself saying, though her voice seemed to echo weirdly as if through a tunnel. Krista's gentle blue eyes looked worried, as though she sensed something of Megan's distress but couldn't understand it. Felicia, too, was obviously sizing Megan up, and Megan raised her brows high in an automatic response of challenge. Let her find fault with the exotic coloring, the borrowed suit.

And yet she couldn't help staring at Krista, comparing her with herself, marveling at how two young women of about the same age could be so different. Krista's calm was not a facade. She truly was as serene as Megan had always wished to be. Her blood clearly was not tormented with the passions that boiled through Megan's veins. One look at her placid blue eyes and her quiescent, thin lips and you knew *she* would never find herself half-naked amid tumbled sheets with a man who didn't, and never would, love her....

"We just wanted to confirm about tonight, Ford," Felicia was saying, having finally completed her survey of Megan and turned her back to her. "I'm going out early myself, so I wanted to be sure you're going to pick Krista up at eight."

"That's the plan," Ford responded lightly, seemingly undisturbed by Felicia's peremptory tone. "If it suits Kris."

Krista nodded, apparently surprised that he should even ask. Megan wondered if Krista would ever even dream of finding her mother's plan unsuitable. Probably not. Megan had seen many girls like her at the convent school, girls who knew that their mothers had their lives mapped out carefully and who had only to follow the rules in order to reach their glittering futures.

Megan, whose own future was a virgin land, over-grown and exotic, waiting to be tamed by her own hand, had told herself she pitied these girls. There were no surprises in store for them, she had consoled herself fiercely. But was her way really better? Yes, there were beautiful discoveries in her world—but there were dangers, too. Dangers like treacherous Tony Ford.

"Oh, and I thought we might invite Megan to join us, Kris," Ford was continuing, his voice elaborately casual. "She's in town for just one night, and I have some more details to go over with her. Would you mind?"

Felicia's frown was more obvious than good breeding should have allowed, but if Krista disliked the idea she didn't show it. She smiled warmly at both Megan and Ford. "Of course not. I'd love it. You'll like the play, Miss Farrell. We're having a wonderful Shakespeare revival this year, and the critics say this one is particularly good."

"Please—not Miss Farrell," Megan corrected automatically. "Megan. And thank you, but I'm a little tired. I think I'll just go back to the hotel—"

"I'm sorry, Megan, but I'm going to have to insist." Ford sounded amused. "Being tired is another luxury you can't afford in the business world. You still haven't heard my plans for Memory Lane, and, after all, your job does depend on them."

She met his eyes and saw that their green depths held a challenge. "All right, then," she said, irony thick in her voice. "I suppose that makes it an offer I can't refuse. I'm sure it will be a lovely evening."

He smiled wryly, and she quickly looked away so that he wouldn't read the fear in her eyes. How *was* she going to live through the evening? How would she be able to endure watching the man who was almost her lover as he tenderly squired another young woman?

And not just *any* woman. Krista Kelly. The woman who—she could hardly believe it herself—the woman who was her sister.

CHAPTER FOUR

HER HALF SISTER, to be more precise.

As she sat on the edge of the bed in the Plaza Hotel, Megan stared in the mirror. But she wasn't seeing the reflection of her evening dress. Her eyes were focused on a spot much farther away, on a scene from the past. . . .

Five years ago. She had been only eighteen, only six months out of the convent high school, only six months free of Sister Margarite. That summer she had worked as a tour guide, sweltering in voluminous antebellum gowns, smiling graciously as she led groups through one of the plantation houses along the Mississippi River. It had been hard work for little pay, but she hadn't cared. Her only goal for the past ten years had been to save enough money to hire a private detective.

And finally she had enough. The assignment she gave him was simple. Find out who had, almost nineteen years before, met the black-haired real-estate secretary Melissa Farrell and fathered one Megan Patricia Farrell.

The man hadn't seemed shocked by Megan's tawdry story—her first welcome hint that Sister Margarite's attitude didn't truly reflect the world's feelings. Nor had he seemed intimidated by Megan's lack of leads.

She did know that it had probably been a brief affair. Megan remembered certain sighing remarks that now seemed to hint at a short, fleeting flame. He had probably not been from New Orleans. And he must have been wealthy. He'd supported her mother. At seven, Megan had begun to wonder where their income came from, and her mother had simply answered, "From your father." The nuns had said the same thing when, after her mother died, she'd asked who paid for her room and board. "Your father."

But that was all. No secreted love letters had surfaced. No locks of hair, no pictures, not even a matchbook memento to lead the way. She had hardly dared to hope the detective would be able to uncover the truth.

When he brought back the folder, less than a month later, she had opened it with trembling hands. She had lived so long with the question—suddenly she wondered whether she would be able to live as easily with the answer.

First there was the name. Patrick Kelly. She'd stared at it a long time. Patrick Kelly. There was no question it was the right name. Somehow the detective had got hold of the checks and traced them. They came from the Chadbourne & Kelly lawyers in New York, and were debited to Patrick Kelly's private account.

Nineteen years ago Patrick Kelly had spent the winter in New Orleans. He had been working on a real estate deal and had used the firm for which Melissa Farrell had worked. Megan's detective had tracked down the other secretaries, who had eagerly remembered their suspicions about the handsome Patrick Kelly and the black-haired Melissa.

So now Megan knew. But the folder had held one last, devastating piece of information. An obituary. Patrick Kelly, New York businessman, had died two years earlier of a heart attack in his Central Park penthouse. He was survived by his widow, Felicia Kelly, and their daughter, the beautiful Krista Kelly.

Megan's heart had hammered at her breast. No! She couldn't, wouldn't accept it. Had she come this far, only to find she'd been chasing a ghost? Short of going straight to New York, there had been only one more lead in the detective's folder. Patrick Kelly had been in partnership with a man named Ashton Hartford Chadbourne II, now also deceased. But Chadbourne's estranged wife, Natalie Chadbourne, was living right here in New Orleans, the owner of an antique store called Memory Lane.

And so, though she'd never told Natalie the truth, Megan's appearance at her store that day five years ago had not been coincidence. She had come to see what she could find out about Patrick Kelly and his other, his legitimate daughter—the girl who was, incredibly, her sister.

But Natalie had not talked much about the old days, when she'd lived in New York and been part of the Chadbourne & Kelly dynasty. She had run away from that life twenty years before, and the few details she'd let spill about her life in the Chadbourne household had not been pleasant.

Gradually, as Megan grew more fond of the feisty old lady and her funny little store, she had realized she wanted no part of Chadbourne & Kelly, either. She had been looking for a sense of home, a sense of family—and with Natalie she had finally found that. As for Patrick Kelly . . . she already knew that her father was the kind of man who, beyond making monetary payments, could ignore his own flesh and blood. That, she had told herself bitterly, was all she needed to know.

And yet, here she was. Her eyes refocused on the mirror, bringing back her reflection. The wide gray eyes were searching. Did she look anything like Krista Kelly? Did the two young women share any heritage from their errant father? Did the secret blood tie betray itself in the shape of an eye, the curve of a smile?

Megan shook her head slowly. No, there was nothing, however wishfully she might search. The two half sisters couldn't have been more different—dark and light, vibrant and pale, vigorous and serene. Their mothers' genes, and their vastly different upbringing, had effectively erased any similarities that might have been born in them.

Aware that it was irrational, she tried not to be so disappointed. She shook herself mentally, trying to throw off the sticky cobwebs of the past. She had not sought out the Kellys herself. She had never pressed any claim on them. And she never would.

She just had to get through tonight....

At least tonight the social distinctions wouldn't be as obvious. At least tonight she wouldn't have to wear a borrowed dress to the theater.

She surveyed her reflection with some satisfaction. She'd washed the mousse out of her hair and let the black curls fall in natural abandon around her shoulders. And her gown couldn't have been more appropriate for an evening on Broadway if Felicia Kelly had picked it out herself.

Most importantly, it *fit*. No more too-tight bodices. She couldn't have endured another single minute of feeling overripe and bosomy next to the gamine Krista Kelly. Thank goodness she had packed a couple of the vintage dresses she'd acquired through the store.

Occasionally customers brought in antique clothes, hoping to sell them. The real beauties—the Worths, the Vionnets, the Schiaparellis—were beyond her budget, but she had learned a lot about restoring fabrics and had picked up a few good things.

This was one of her favorites, a loose turquoise silk sheath fringed with overlapping rows of beads that shone with the blue-green iridescence of peacock feathers when she moved. The color never seemed exactly the same twice, and it played on her gray eyes like a kaleidoscope.

One last look in the mirror—damn, even without makeup her cheeks and lips were a high-strung scarlet. A ragged sigh of mingled exasperation and anxiety, a tingling descent in the elevator cage, and suddenly she was in the lobby.

"Megan!" Krista found her instantly and was gliding forward. Megan sighed inwardly as she took in Krista's delicately chiseled features and compared them to the flushed cheeks and bee-stung lips she'd seen in the mirror. And her clothes—Krista was wearing a simple black dress, with an off-the-shoulder neckline, a belted waist and a full skirt. In her swinging colored beads, Megan felt like a cheap dance-hall darling.

In an instant Ford appeared behind Krista. He laid his strong hands on Krista's bare shoulders, and she dropped her head casually back against his chest.

"Hi, there," Krista murmured, smiling up into his chin. "I told you I'd find her first."

The casual tone bewildered Megan. How could Krista appear so unmoved by those hands against her skin? If Ford had touched *her* collarbone that way, the blood would have raced helplessly to the surface. Krista's ivory skin held no flush, and the only sparkle in her eyes appeared to be admiration for Megan's dress.

"Doesn't she look beautiful, Ford? Doesn't that dress look just like a Schiaparelli, or a..."

From his vantage point above Krista's shoulder, Ford's eyes ran the length of Megan's body, snagging almost unwillingly at the subtle shimmer where her breast curved the fabric toward the light. "Those names don't mean anything to me, Krista," he said, looking up again finally. "But if you mean it looks expensive, then yes, it certainly does."

Megan felt the flush on her cheeks deepen. Was she just imagining an implied criticism?

"You should have seen it when I bought it," she said, though she hated herself for explaining. She didn't use Memory Lane's money to buy her dresses, and therefore it was no business of his. "The silk was so badly stained it was brown, and half the beads were missing. The lady who sold it to me was on her way to the Goodwill box. It probably cost less than your socks."

Her vehemence obviously amused him. His green eyes were uptilted, and the line between his cheekbone and his jaw grew a fraction deeper, as though he repressed a smile.

"What's wrong with my socks?" He looked at his feet in mock dismay. "I knew I paid too much for them. Pure silk Tibetan designer socks are vastly overrated."

"Oh, Ford," Krista frowned prettily and slapped at the hand that held her shoulder. "Don't tease Megan so. She doesn't know you as well as I do. She won't know what to think." She shook her head helplessly. "I barely understand him myself. He thinks the strangest things are funny."

Megan gave Ford a cold smile. "Oh, I think I understand Ford's jokes better than he realizes," she said dryly.

"Well, then," Ford responded, lifting one dark brow and finally releasing Krista, "since we all understand one another, why don't we get on to the theater? Despite Felicia's best efforts, Krista has never learned to be fashionably late."

He held out an arm for each woman, and reluctantly Megan took it, if only to avoid attracting attention by refusing. It was warm, tightly muscled and palpably sensual—some vibrant, masculine potion might be coursing through it instead of blood. Touching Ford was like being forced to hold her hand over a flame, and she had to steel herself to keep from ripping it away.

Krista clung easily to his other side, still chattering as they descended the steps toward the waiting black limousine.

"It's just that I love the theater. I can't imagine missing part of a terrific play just to impress people. Not if you really like theater. Though, of course, mother says she just goes because she needs somewhere to wear her gowns." Krista laughed, a musical sound, but she sobered quickly, as if realizing it hadn't been especially nice to poke fun at her mother. "I don't think she means it, though. She just enjoys saying outrageous things."

Megan nodded noncommittally, but she suspected that Felicia Kelly had meant every word. Painted and lacquered women usually had little interest in anything but their own looks.

Even so, you couldn't expect her own daughter to agree, so Megan simply nodded again. But as Ford handed her into the leather seat of the limo, he caught her eye with a wicked smile. *She meant it,* the look said, *and you know it, too.*

As she stared at him, his mahogany head bent low to clear the glossy black roof, it was as if they spoke to each other without words. Their gaze didn't waver, though Krista kept talking, and Megan could almost hear him inviting her to enter into a conspiracy to protect Krista from her shallow mother. Megan shook her head, confused by the intensity of the feeling.

Then he climbed in beside her, pressing the long, hot length of his body next to hers, hip to hip, and desire rose up in clouds around her, interfering with communication.

As the limo smoothly pulled away from the curb, she folded her trembling hands in her lap and shook herself mentally. Stop it, she screamed at herself. Stop it *now*.

It wasn't the physical desire that terrified her. Though regrettable, it made perfect sense to be attracted to Ford Chadbourne. He was gorgeous—tall, dark, handsome, every time-honored cliché in the book.

No, what frightened her was that she continued to imagine a psychic link with him. The same sense of Destiny that had made her believe she'd fallen in love with Tony Ford after only one week still vibrated in the air between them. The fatal difference was that now she knew he *wasn't* Mr. Right. Now she knew he was instead the ultimate Mr. Wrong.

It made a sort of poetic justice, then, that their tickets should be for *Romeo and Juliet*. The chandeliers were already dimming into a winking twilight as they sidled into their fifth-row-center seats. Though she knew etiquette demanded that Ford sit between them, Megan managed to maneuver Krista into the middle position. She couldn't bear the thought of Ford's long arm resting next to hers, his strong hand dangling near her lap.

Even so, it was well into the second act before she relaxed enough to enjoy the play. Then, safely wedged between Krista's gentle smile and the aloof magnificence of a bejeweled elderly lady, she gave herself over to the magic of Shakespeare.

It wasn't until the final curtain, when she tasted the warm salt of her own tears, that she remembered Ford consciously. Embarrassed, she wiped the tears away and darted a glance in his direction. His profile was impassive. Obviously he hadn't seen her tears. And unlike her, he was completely unmoved.

But what else should she have expected? She sniffed quietly. This wasn't Tony Ford. There *was* no Tony Ford. This was Ford Chadbourne, and even Shakespeare couldn't move his heart. He didn't have one.

The night seemed even colder after the crowded warmth of the theater, and Megan was glad to see Ford's limousine standing at the curb. She shivered, wishing she'd been able to buy an opera cloak to go with her foolish dress. Or wishing she were home, where even the coldest winter was kinder than this.

Had he interpreted her shiver as a plea for his touch? Probably—it was the kind of ultrafeminine game debutantes played. His arm slipped quickly around her cold shoulders, and the crystal beads tinkled faintly as he rubbed her upper arm.

She shut her eyes against the explosion of emotion that burst when their bodies touched. It was ridiculous—she hadn't forgotten for one instant how much she hated him—but his touch was like being "touched" by dynamite. Just when it seemed that the sickening, melting feeling would distort her bones, he let go.

"Better?" He looked at her clinically. "That damn dress is beautiful all right—but not very practical. Next time buy something with long sleeves. New York isn't New Orleans."

She narrowed her eyes and pulled as far away as the thronging crowd would allow. "I don't expect there to be a next time," she bit out, the words an angry whisper.

"Why don't we just get down to business, and then I can go back to New Orleans where my clothes are quite suitable!"

"All right." Unmoved by her outburst, he nodded at the chauffeur, who opened the limo's back door. With a nod of thanks, Krista stepped in.

Megan moved to follow her, but Ford caught her arm. "No. Krista's going home. You and I have business to discuss."

Megan looked, horrified, from Krista's smile to Ford's dark eyes.

"But I thought..." What *had* she thought? Earlier, she had dreaded the idea of spending the evening with one of the Kellys, but already she had come to feel at ease with Krista. She instinctively recognized the young woman's sweet nature and now realized that she'd been counting on it to serve as a buffer between herself and Ford. The truth was she was afraid to be alone with him. She didn't know whether she was afraid they would end up fighting or making love—but she knew she was afraid. Desperately afraid.

"But you haven't had any dinner, have you, Krista?" It was a last-ditch effort, and she wasn't surprised when Krista laughed.

"Don't tell mother, but I always eat *before* I go to the theater. I just get too hungry to wait. But Ford's going to take you to dinner, I think. Aren't you, Ford?"

Ford nodded and leaned over to kiss her goodbye. "Sleep tight, Kris," he said, patting her cheek.

"I will," she said. "'Bye, Megan. Take her somewhere chic, Ford. Show her how great New York is, and maybe she'll come back to see us."

And then, in a flash of reflected marquee lights, the limo was gone. Ford was flagging a taxi, managing, with some indefinable air of authority, to attract the first one that drove by.

When the taxi stopped in front of an apartment building across from Central Park, Megan leaned forward with surprise.

"Dinner?" She spoke the word frostily.

"We're having dinner at my apartment," he answered and pulled her from the cab. "We'll have move privacy here."

But privacy was the last thing she wanted, her mind cried as they entered the lobby. She needed crowds, waiters, menus to hide behind . . . not a tête-à-tête in his living room . . . or did he have the bedroom in mind?

And yet part of her was curious, in spite of her nerves. This was where he lived. Would it tell her anything about him? At the moment, here in the lobby, she saw only the obvious—like everything else about him, it spoke of money.

But his apartment surprised her. It was expensive, all right, thick with polished cherrywood furniture, muffled with priceless Turkish carpets and gleaming with Waterford table lamps. But it was small. It was warm. It was full of books and pictures. It was not a showplace. It was a home.

"Do you like it?"

Shutting the door, he hung his dark coat on the brass hat stand and stood, dwarfing the small foyer, awaiting her answer.

She surveyed the room slowly, trying to appear indifferent, but the skin on the back of her neck was prickling, raising tiny goose bumps that then cascaded down her back like cold water. Like it? It was as if she had stepped into a haunted room—haunted by the ghost of Tony Ford.

Against all reason she could smell Tony here, in the piney warmth of the crackling fire and the subtle musk of dark wood scent. It was as though he had just stepped away—a book lay on the table, and the worn leather of the armchair still retained the impression of someone's body.

She shut her eyes, trying to block out the sensations. She mustn't keep slipping back into this fantasy. She was like a drugged sleeper trying to awaken.

She gritted her teeth, fighting the feeling, and opened her eyes. "Very nice."

Did she imagine that he looked disappointed? Certainly his green eyes grew more hooded, but he didn't challenge her. Instead he moved farther into the room.

"We can work after we eat," he said and turned toward an arched alcove, where a round black-lacquered table had been set for two with vermeil flatware and gold-and-black-rimmed china. One yellow gardenia floated in a shallow vermeil bowl, fragmented and reflected in the two empty, brilliant-cut crystal goblets. The effect was spare, masculine—yet quite beautiful.

Like Ford himself. For a moment she was unable to wrench her eyes from his face. The ghost of Tony Ford had touched him, too. She could see again that his mouth was full and generous, belying the arrogance of his strong, hard jaw. And was there really cruelty behind those eyes of hunter green? Oh, surely not . . . She was slipping again, ever deeper, losing touch with the anger she had clutched to her heart for two days now.

With a small smile he held out a gold, silk-covered chair, and she entered the alcove and sat. Her blood had ceased its roaring in her ears. Now she was preternaturally quiet, as if she swam, alone and deep, in a moonlit ocean.

He sat, too, and magically a servant appeared with soup and wine. Obediently, but almost unaware, she drank the warm, creamy mixture from the golden spoon and then she sipped the cool, amber liquid from the goblet. The diamond pattern pressed like a cold brand into her lips, and the wine burned a hot path down her throat. Still she didn't surface from her dark submersion.

They didn't speak, except of trivial matters that didn't ripple the surface of her trance, though their eyes met often, over raised rainbowed crystal, and above tiny forks that held small white morsels of lobster.

Then the lobster was gone, and black and gold coffee cups were before them, steam curling up to lick moistly at her face.

Suddenly, through her haze, she saw Ford frown, his brows drawing together. Confused, she glanced up, and saw that his servant had brought something else, something that finally awakened her, shooting her, confused and gasping, from her deep trance into the cold, stinging air again. It was the brown folder she'd seen in Jim Brackett's lap earlier that day. It was Memory Lane reduced to a row of soulless figures.

She gripped the cup, welcoming the bracing heat that scalded her palms. So that had been his plan. An intimate dinner to lull her into a less combative mood. Well, he would see.

"Good. Business." She arranged her face poker-playing straight and kept her voice flat. "The dinner was delicious, but it's been a long day, and I was hoping we would get to this soon."

"Were you?" He leaned back in his chair, his eyes hooded again. "Odd—I could have sworn you'd forgotten all about it."

She laughed shortly and straightened her back. "Forgotten? Hardly! It may be trivial to you but not to me. I have a strong feeling that's my future you're holding in that folder."

He tapped a long forefinger on the closed cover. "Oh, not anything that dramatic. After all, your job is guaranteed by Natalie's will, isn't it?"

She narrowed her eyes at the hint of sarcasm in his deep voice. This was beginning to look like a game of cat and mouse, and she disliked being the mouse.

"As long as Memory Lane stays open, it is. But I've read the will, too. We both know you could lock the doors any day, and I'd be on the streets." She leaned forward, the crystal beads clicking against the lacquered table. "So let's get to the point, Ford. You're obviously not happy with the store. You made that painfully clear this afternoon. Why don't you just tell me what you intend to do?"

His fingers ceased their tapping. "All right. It's pretty simple. First, I have no interest in closing down the business. That's expensive property—there's no reason to waste it."

Megan's breath came out in an audible sigh. She had been so sure he intended to do just that.

"But I don't intend to be satisfied with this kind of profit, either." He opened the folder and frowned at the numbers.

She jumped in eagerly. "I think we can do a little better," she said. "The customers are finally beginning to trust my advice. They got so used to Natalie, you see, and I'm rather young, and they weren't sure I understood the merchandise as well as she did. But it's getting better...." She heard the overeager note in her voice and eased down a bit. She pushed her curls back behind her ears and laid her hands on the table.

"Of course, Memory Lane will never make as much money as a regular retail store. It's hard to acquire our kind of merchandise, and it doesn't move as quickly. A book can sit on the shelves for years sometimes before the right customer comes along. But when that customer comes, he really wants his book, and he'll pay for it." She laughed. "It's wonderful, really, to see how thrilled someone can be to find a rare book."

She stopped and smiled over at him, dimly aware that he wasn't smiling back. But she was too caught up in her relief about keeping the store to realize what his stony look could mean. "I know I'm babbling, but I really do love the place. And Natalie always said—"

As though the name had been an obscenity, he cut her off roughly, his eyes flashing. "I'm not interested in what Natalie always said. She may have been content to make very little profit, but I'm not. That's why we're planning to change Memory Lane to a boutique."

Her mouth must have been open, because her throat was too dry to swallow. "A *what*?"

"A women's boutique." His eyes were hard. "We'll still call it Memory Lane, but it will carry women's clothes. Old-fashioned clothes, I understand. Like the one you're wearing." His gaze didn't drop an inch but kept hold of hers, unwavering. "Except that they'll be copies, of course. The merchandise must be something you can order by the dozen, or else you'll fall right back into the trap you're in now. We need high turnover in a high-rent district like the French Quarter."

He riffled through the papers and handed her a set of pages filled with black typing. She bent her head, but her mind was so scrambled she couldn't read.

"What is this?" Her voice was strangled.

"It's the market study I commissioned for that property. It explains everything—why Memory Lane doesn't work the way it is, and why a boutique is a better idea." He leaned forward and tapped the top of the page. "It even shows you how much we can expect to net in the first two months of the new business. Read it, Megan. I think you'll see it's a wise move."

"Why?" Her voice rose like the scream of a boiling steam kettle. "Because it will make more *money*? What about all the beautiful, unique things we have there now? Don't they matter? Doesn't anything matter to you but money?"

"Don't be ridiculous." He took the paper out of her stiff fingers and laid it back into the folder. "Memory Lane is a business not a museum. Of course it's money that matters. It's money that keeps the damned thing from going bankrupt, or are you too naive to understand that?"

She balled her hands into fists and pressed them in her lap. "Don't you dare patronize me! Memory Lane is not anywhere near going bankrupt and you know it."

He sighed. "It's also not coming anywhere near *these* figures, either! And it never will, if you continue to run it with your schoolgirl sentimentality."

The arrogance of it took her breath away. Their angry eyes locked and she knew hers were as stormy as his. She could hear the hostility in his harsh breathing and the violent pounding of her heart.

He was so unbelievably slick. It hadn't taken him long to get around poor Natalie's will. His mother had tried to ensure that Memory Lane would be tended by someone who loved it. But Natalie had been no match for this cold-blooded money machine. Her eyes burning, Megan choked back a sob of frustration.

She longed to lash out, but she had promised Natalie that she would do everything she could to protect Memory Lane. And besides, she loved the store, too. Memory Lane and Natalie had come as close to being a home and family as anything had since the day her mother died. Who was Ford Chadbourne to turn her out of her home?

By god, she wouldn't go. He thought he was smarter than she just because he had inherited a fistful of money. How vain! Any fool with ambition and no scruples could make money.

She took a deep, burning breath. If it was money he wanted, that was what he would get. She was far from a fool—she was Patrick Kelly's daughter, even if Kelly hadn't bothered to acknowledge it. Surely she had inherited some of his genes. Even burdened by scruples she could squeeze enough profits out of Memory Lane to dazzle Ford Chadbourne thoroughly.

"But suppose I *can*?" she asked, a hint of defiance seeping into her voice. "Suppose I can bring in a profit like the one you wanted from your boutique? Suppose you've underestimated Memory Lane? Suppose you've underestimated *me*?"

A chill frosted his words. "I haven't."

"But what if you have? Don't I deserve a chance? I didn't know money was the bottom line—it wasn't for Natalie. Now that I *do*, I'm sure I can meet your target."

Her heart was tight in her chest. It sounded dangerously like begging—but at least she wasn't begging for herself. It was for the store. And for Natalie. He just had to agree.

He was frowning, but at least he hadn't cut her off. The hesitation gave her hope.

"Didn't you say two months? Well, give me those same two months, and see if I can't bring you the same profit. If I don't, you've only lost sixty days, and—and I'll agree to work in your boutique with no complaints." She knew the argument was thin. What did he care whether she stayed on or not? If anything, he'd probably be glad to see her go.

But surely he could see that her plan was fair. Or did he have any sense of fair play? She swallowed hard. She had to gamble that he did.

"You must see the advantages of my idea," she said sensibly. "You would have to restock completely to change Memory Lane into a boutique. Even liquidating the stock that is there now would be a nuisance. You'd have to buy new fixtures—that's a huge expense. And there's the problem of name recognition. It could take months to build a new following."

She wondered whether he believed any of this. It was true, and yet somehow she couldn't believe the money meant everything to him. What was a few hundred thousand dollars to the Widget King? It must be something else, something more personal. Perhaps he just wanted to rub out what Natalie had left behind—just out of spite. The thought stiffened her resolve, and she continued her one-sided debate with renewed vigor.

"And market research has been wrong before, you know. It's hardly an exact science. Suppose they misjudged this time—suppose your boutique failed? There must be two dozen boutiques in the French Quarter already. Why risk all that money before you give Memory Lane one last chance?"

He had been listening patiently, but now his fingers were tapping again. The sound was heartening—already she had learned that it indicated he was wrestling with an internal dilemma.

He narrowed his eyes and looked hard into hers. She tried to keep her anger damped down. Her chest was still heaving from her earlier outburst, and the crystals winked under the chandelier. She breathed shallowly and sipped her coffee.

When he spoke, it was with an inscrutable calm. "Let's be specific. Either you make a ten-thousand-dollar profit in the next two months or you agree to work at the boutique without complaint."

She coughed as the coffee slipped toward her airpipe. Ten thousand dollars! She had been too agitated to see the figures on the research report, and the numbers hit her like a punch in the stomach. Easing the cup into its saucer, she did a few panicked calculations. Ten thousand dollars! Memory Lane didn't net that in *six* months! She would have to triple her profits....

One corner of his mouth was curled in something that maddeningly hinted at a smirk. Obviously he had intended the number to be a shock. He was probably hoping she'd stammer some excuse and back down.

Instead she cleared her throat softly and smiled. "Right."

Lacing his fingers together, he leaned back in his chair. His hair was brilliant under the lights. "And if you *do*?"

"What do you mean?"

"I mean if you *do* manage to net a profit of ten thousand dollars, what do you expect from me? Do you expect me to back off entirely and never concern myself with Memory Lane again, no matter how little money it makes?"

"Of course not." She shook her head, and the curls tumbled back over her shoulders. "I just expect you to acknowledge that you were wrong about Memory Lane. And to allow me to continue running it *my* way, as long as profits are maintained."

He rubbed the tips of his index fingers across his lips thoughtfully. "You would have to maintain your inventory, too. The profits would be figured after restocking."

She lowered her lids, veiling the flame of triumph that flared there. He was considering it. "Isn't that the way all businesses are run?"

"All of *my* businesses are," he answered smoothly.

"Either accept the deal or decline it," she snapped and stood up, the beads of her dress clicking emphatically, "but don't insult me. I won't stand for it. There are other jobs."

"Sorry," he said, not sounding so at all. Pushing his chair back, he, too, stood up. "Fair enough, then. It's a deal. Two months. You make ten thousand dollars by, say, midnight on Mardi Gras—and you win. One penny less and Memory Lane will be a boutique by Easter."

She swallowed hard, her heart again racing in her breast. It couldn't be done! But it must. "Agreed."

He held out his hand. "Deal."

She slipped her fingers into his. With the first spark of contact, his hand tightened. She pulled away instinctively, trying to release herself, but he held on. Their hands locked, he drew her toward him slowly, with intense concentration, much as he might reel in a difficult catch.

"Actually," he said with dangerous softness, "it might be interesting watching you try to turn this business around."

Watching me squirm, you mean. She could tell by his relaxed features that he didn't believe for a minute she could succeed. Anger flared in her again, burning away her own doubts. It just might be fun to show him how wrong he was.

Again she tried to wriggle her hand loose, but his grip was like a vise. Minutely, with smooth inexorability, he was easing her toward him. She could feel the approaching heat of his body. As she resisted the pull, she stumbled slightly, but her reluctant feet somehow took her all the way, to where the silk of her dress rubbed against the lapels of his jacket.

"Well, then. Shall we seal it with a kiss?" His voice was a warm murmur, and she felt herself sway into his embrace. Her racing blood stung, seeming to leave tiny pinpricks up and down her neck.

For a moment she might have been back in the French Quarter, back with her wonderful Tony. She shut her eyes as his sweet, hot breath burned against her cheeks. His shirt smelled just as Tony always had, of warm starch and an undeniable virility, and she breathed it in deeply. His arms slid down her spine, as though following a familiar course, and rested in the soft hollow just below her waist.

"Meggie." His voice was warm, too—Tony's voice. "Meggie."

But he wasn't Tony. His lips were only a heartbeat away when she pulled back. Her thundering blood roared its protest through her veins. She could hardly hear herself speak.

"Perhaps I didn't make myself clear. You'll get your money. Every cent. But I am *not* part of the deal."

CHAPTER FIVE

As soon as her plane touched down in New Orleans she felt better. It was raining and cold, but it was home. Hoisting her bag over her shoulder, she joined the line to the doors eagerly. After her ordeal in New York this was heaven.

It was almost three o'clock, but she decided to stop in at Memory Lane anyway. She climbed into Natalie's old Subaru and worked her way through to Jackson Square, which, in spite of the rain, was thick with people.

Her jubilation at this sign of a thriving tourist season fought with her impatience as she downshifted the clutch and waited for the pedestrians to splash through the crossing. The car growled underfoot, as though it sensed her mood, and she almost laughed out loud. A growing thrill of exhilaration was replacing her anxiety. Apparently she had inherited more from Patrick Kelly than she'd realized. A good business contest was not intimidating. It was downright exciting.

Becky's brown eyes grew wide as Megan entered the shop. She was ringing up a sale, so she contented herself with the cryptic, "Hey, there. You're mighty pink in the cheeks. Do I hear bells?"

Smiling automatically at the spectacled man who stood at the desk, Megan scanned his purchases. He'd bought every Hemingway they had. She made a mental note—Hemingway was hard to replace.

"Bells?" She shook her head at Becky's romanticism. "Sorry. Not the kind you're thinking of." She tapped the top book in the stack, a copy of *For Whom the Bell Tolls.* "This kind, perhaps. The kind that tolls for thee. Or rather, for me."

"Rats." Becky grinned at her customer, who looked impatient. "That'll be a hundred and twenty-five fifty. You got some fine books. One of these is a first edition." She ripped off the receipt and swiveled to Megan. "Tolling bells, huh? So what went wrong?"

The man wrote out his check quickly, ignoring Becky's chitchat, and left without even a nod goodbye.

Groaning, Becky slipped the check into the drawer. "Have you ever noticed that people who read Hemingway have no sense of humor? Give me a good Scott Fitzgerald fan any day. Now tell me all about it. I'm just sick with curiosity. A whirlwind trip to New York to meet a millionaire. What could go wrong?"

Megan laughed. It was good to be home. She perched on the edge of the desk, eyed the other customers to be sure they didn't need help and proceeded to tell the whole maddening story.

When she finished, Becky sighed. "Oh, hell's bells. I knew he was too good to be true. Men shouldn't be that gorgeous. It rots their souls or something. I just knew it."

"You did not, you fraud," Megan expostulated. "You were practically pushing me out the door and into his arms, remember? All that talk about Mr. Right?"

"Well, is it a crime to hope?" Becky's mouth twisted in a wry grin. "It's hope that keeps us going. How else could I drag myself out on all these pathetic dates? Hope is the only thing that keeps me from joining that convent of yours."

Megan slid off the desk and smoothed down her skirt. "Hogwash. What keeps you from becoming a nun, Becky, is that you're the most outrageous hedonist in this city, and they wouldn't have you on a platter."

"That, too," Becky admitted, laughing, as another customer approached. "That, too."

This customer needed help, so Megan went off in search of pre-World War I postcards for him. With a little extra effort she managed to unearth about fifty dollars worth of cards. Not bad for a half hour's work. But she quickly calculated the cost of the cards, salaries, the overhead . . . Suddenly weary she dropped onto the nearest armchair. It would take a year to clear ten thousand dollars at this rate.

Becky must have been doing similar calculations. When the last customer had exited into the twilight and Megan was bent over the bank deposit, Becky wandered casually to the bookshelves.

"My brother's birthday is coming up soon," she threw out airily, "and I've decided it's time for him to have a new hobby. He's going to have to learn to read something besides *Playboy*. I was thinking maybe a full set of Dickens . . . or maybe this Sherlock Holmes set. . . ."

With a rueful smile Megan watched Becky study the shelves, obviously searching for the most expensive books. She'd already named two of their best sets.

"I've got an idea," Megan told her back. "How about that illuminated Bible over there?" It was the most expensive thing in the store. "It costs a fortune, but if you're trying to reform him it's probably worth it. And since, if I recall correctly, his birthday isn't for another *nine* months, you could put it on lay-away."

Becky turned and wrinkled her nose in a sheepish smile. "Okay, okay. So I'm not the most subtle person in the world. But it's a good idea anyway. I've got a great-uncle who's into cartography and an aunt who will buy any book as long as it's exactly twelve inches tall and has a certain shade of red leather binding. We'll buy so much stuff this Ford creep will think you're a genius."

For a moment Megan didn't answer, her voice having been swept away by a flood of gratitude. It was a shame she couldn't accept the generous, loyal offer. But she couldn't. She caught a glimpse of her profile in the mirror. Her cheeks were pink, her full lips firmly set, and her chin lifted high. She might be a Kelly—but she was also a Farrell, and that stood for something, too. She was willing to work herself into a decline to win this bet if necessary, but she was not willing to sacrifice her ethics. She would win, and she would do it fair and square.

"Thanks anyway, Becky," she said, her voice firm. "It's incredibly sweet, and like all sweet things, it's tempting. But I don't need to stoop to cheating to win this bet. Memory Lane is a terrific store, and it can succeed on its own merits."

Becky slid the Sherlock Holmes volume back into place reluctantly and faced Megan squarely. "I know that, honey. He's just raised the bar awfully high, you know?" Her usually pert voice was almost somber. "Megan, honey, you must see that it's not fair—it isn't meant to be. He wants to enjoy watching you fail, the creep."

"Maybe." Unexpectedly Megan's heart twisted. It hurt to hear it put so bluntly, though Becky's cynicism only echoed her own thoughts. Dropping her pen, she stared blankly toward the bay window, where car lights crawled slowly by, fracturing the curtain of rain. Where had her earlier lust for the battle gone? Now she just felt hollow.

"But if I win by sinking to his level, that isn't winning at all," she finished in a low voice. "There's something even more important than the store at stake here."

Becky nodded slowly, but Becky had been born to pride and privilege. She didn't know what it meant to fight for them.

But Megan Farrell did. And by god she *was* a fighter. Totaling the last figures rapidly, she licked the bank envelope and then ran her fist along the back, sealing the wet glue.

"Oh, listen to us, for heaven's sake. We sound like the oracles at Delphi. Let's lighten up," Megan said, slipping the deposit into her purse. "Frankly I think we're both just hungry."

She suddenly realized how true that was. Too keyed up to stomach airplane food, she hadn't eaten all day. She eased her arms into her trench coat and flipped the window sign to Closed.

"I say we go get in line at K-Paul's," she said, opening the door briskly. "I think a martini in a jelly jar would lift our spirits considerably."

THREE WEEKS LATER a busload of martinis wouldn't have helped cheer her up. Business had been terrible. Every customer who came in asked for something she didn't have. And perversely, they all wanted the same things! If she'd had about two dozen copies of *Uncle Tom's Cabin* and about a hundred copies of *Gone With The Wind*, she would have been rich. As it was, she would be hard-pressed to come up with February's rent.

Even worse, she had worked alone every day for the past three weeks, and she was beat. It might not have been financially prudent, but she had hired Becky for the weekend. What luxury it was to loll around her little carriage house in her blue flannel robe, her feet bare and her hair as wild as a gypsy's! Relishing the freedom of no nylons, not even a bra, she put mandolin music on the stereo, a steam kettle on the stove and herself on the sofa. Just a quick rest, just until the water boiled, and then she'd tackle the merchandise she had brought home.

The next thing she knew it was dark. Not just the deep gray of heavy rain, but the black void of night. It must be six, at least, and she must have slept for two full hours. The stereo speakers were making strange popping noises, and the steam kettle was sizzling, the water long boiled away.

"Drat," she whispered groggily, sitting up and rubbing her eyes. This was all Ford Chadbourne's fault, his fault that she was physically overworked and emotionally overwrought. She scanned the living room, remembering how tiny it had looked with him in it, how pleased she had been by his approval, how soft her bed had been under them.

She stood up forcefully, clearing the images from her mind. And it was definitely his fault that she couldn't enter her own home anymore without thinking of him, almost seeing him, feeling his hands all over again....

Well, tonight would be different. Tonight she had a date of sorts. Harry was coming at seven-thirty to take her to Arnaud's. She grinned. Harry's jewelry store must be enjoying better business than hers. Her scanty income couldn't have handled Arnaud's—these days Popeye's fried chicken constituted splurging.

The telephone rang just as she reached the kitchen. Tucking it under her chin, she stretched to switch off the burner.

"Hello?"

"Hi. It's me." Becky's voice sounded upbeat, and Megan said a silent prayer that it meant she had sold something *very* expensive. But Becky dashed that dream quickly. "Don't get your hopes up. No business to speak of. A couple of hundred."

Megan sighed and shifted the scalded kettle to a cold burner. "Oh well, maybe tomorrow. What is it then? You sound—I don't know—bouncy."

"Just my natural high spirits, I guess," Becky responded gaily. "And, of course, I have a date with a cute guy tonight, and I'm pretty sure he won't turn out to be married, devoted to Mamma or just generally a fly."

Megan smiled wanly and poured herself a Diet Coke. Maybe the caffeine would jolt her back to the land of the living. "I have a date with Harry," she volunteered dryly.

"Well, then, cheer up! Harry may be a little stuck on himself, but at least he's not a fly."

Megan chuckled but didn't commit herself on the point.

"Anyhow, that's not why I'm calling," Becky went on. "Mr. Toby came by with some stuff he wants to sell you. I told him you weren't here, so he said he'd leave it on Natalie's front porch. I think you'd better go get it before the wretched rain starts up."

"Okay." Megan felt a small spark of interest. Mr. Toby, one of Natalie's oldest friends, always had such fascinating things. "Did he say how much he wants for it?"

"Nope. He said you could just make an offer."

Megan grimaced. She hated to buy things that way. Her conscience always demanded that she offer top dollar, and she never came away with the bargains other dealers bragged about.

She wished Becky good luck on her date and hung up. The cola had begun to shoot some energy into her languid veins, and she decided to run out and get the box. Already the sky looked smoky and heavy. The rain couldn't be far off.

Thanking heaven for the obsessive privacy of the Garden District, she scampered down the steep steps in her bare feet and walked carefully across the bricked garden toward the big house. The porch wrapped around the house, so she could reach the package with minimum exposure to the street.

Just imagine what her neighbors would think if they could see her now, hair flying wildly, her robe buttoned high at the neck and belted tightly at the waist but clearly covering only her naked body. She scurried back to her house, holding the box under one arm and clutching the ends of her robe with the other.

Inside, as the rain fell against the windows in silver sheets, she explored Mr. Toby's offerings. She'd been right. The carton was like a treasure box, filled with beautiful things. Where did Mr. Toby get these marvels? She gasped softly as she unrolled an illuminated manuscript page. And where in creation was *she* going to get the money to buy them from him? A leather-bound set of the Elizabethan poets, a stack of pre-World War I New Orleans postcards and, she whooped jubilantly, a *Gone With the Wind*.

But nestled in the bottom was the most wonderful find of all. She picked up the small volume tenderly, sensing its age at once. She turned the brittle, hand-written pages carefully, savoring the smell of well-preserved antiquity.

It turned out to be a packet of letters, a diary written from an American Civil War captain to his infant daughter. Megan lowered herself onto her wicker rocker, flicked on the lamp, and kept reading.

An hour later she closed the book and leaned her head back against the rocker. Slow, warm tears rolled from her eyes as she shut them. She hadn't even realized they were there. Were they for the captain? The last letter had been from the War Department, informing his widow of his death. Or had her tears been for the little girl who would never know the father who had loved her so well? Or had they been for little Meggie, who also had never known her father?

When she was a child, she had always dreamed that someday her father would write her such a letter, filled with love and longing. But reality had been very different. Patrick Kelly had never once acknowledged her existence—unless she counted the convent school tuition and boarding fees. Another hot tear seeped from under her closed lids. Never a personal word.

The rain was moving away now, heading for the Gulf. The heavy drops that had trampled across her roof had given way to a sibilant whispering. The sound was melancholy, and she heard herself sighing along with it.

Her visit to New York had been unsettling in so many ways. Seeing Ford Chadbourne, of course, had been the most obvious. But seeing Krista had opened another whole Pandora's box.

She shifted uneasily in her chair, as though trying to escape the disturbing thoughts.

Until she had met Krista, Megan had believed she had Patrick Kelly neatly pigeonholed. A selfish, irresponsible man who cared only about himself and his money. He hadn't minded leaving behind a woman whose life was wrecked, a little girl who would never know her father.

Such a man was not worth longing for, dreaming about. And so Megan had put her dreams away.

But now she'd seen Krista, and the old longings began to stir. Krista couldn't be so easily dismissed. She was elegant and privileged, yes, but she was also natural and open. It was obvious that Felicia Kelly had not been responsible for those qualities. But how could Patrick Kelly have fathered such sweetness?

Now it was a question that could never be resolved. Patrick Kelly was dead, and with him all hopes of understanding her heritage had died, too. Megan stood up, arching her back to stretch her cramped muscles. Her head ached from unshed tears. Rubbing her brow, she went to the window. She needed fresh air to blow the goblins away.

As she reached to twist the lock, her hands froze. Where she expected to see a moonless black, instead she saw rectangles of honey light. Shutters were open at two of Natalie's windows, spilling light onto the back porch and down into the courtyard. She frowned, her stomach constricting nervously.

Vagrants? Once before she'd had trouble with them. Though the Garden District itself was quiet and exclusive, it was a target for thieves, and owners had to be careful.

She squinted, searching for signs of activity. Surely vagrants wouldn't be so careless as to leave lights burning....

She picked up the telephone, never taking her eyes off the windows, and called the police. The dispatcher promised to send someone immediately. She stood watching another minute and then quietly eased down the steps and across the courtyard. She'd just take a look. It might be kids, maybe even lovers from nearby Tulane

University, and she could run them off with a few threats. It would be a shame for them to get picked up by the police if they weren't really hurting anything.

But on the back porch she hesitated, shivering. She couldn't look awfully threatening right now, barefoot, hair cascading around her shoulders and her fuzzy robe damp from the drizzle. Automatically she checked the big white button near her throat. Maybe she should just go back, change into some jeans and wait for the police.

Retreating, she had just put one cold foot on the first wet step when the door opened behind her.

"Looking for me?"

The ironic tones shot through her like a bullet. She froze, disbelieving, gripping the icy wrought-iron railing so hard her fingers seemed made of ice, too.

She forced herself to turn. He was silhouetted by the light behind him, but she would have known that tall, muscular body anywhere. Her stomach was clenched tight, her pulse drumming erratically. She hated him at that moment for frightening her so.

"What are *you* doing here?" She didn't care if she sounded rude. He should have known it would scare her.

His silhouette shifted. He looked behind him, as if checking, and then leaned against the door frame. "Unless my lawyers have misled me, this *is* my house. Why shouldn't I be here?"

"You didn't tell me you were coming." She felt light-headed, and tried to take a deep breath. Strange how similar anger and desire were. They had the same shaking intensity. She was suddenly, unhappily aware of her dishabille, of her cold breasts outlined by the damp fabric, of her legs peeking through the robe.

"Do I need your permission?" His voice was as cold as the air, and a new spasm of rippling shivers ran over her.

"Of course not. I just didn't know what was going on. The lights—the shutters..." She was stammering like a fool. "Oh, never mind. I just—forget it." She started down the steps.

But through the open door the low chimes of the doorbell arrested her. Oh, no—she had forgotten the police.

She whirled quickly, almost losing her balance on the slick step. "Ford. That's probably... I—I called the police."

This time he froze. "You *what*?"

"When I saw the lights. I didn't know who was here. I called the police...." Her voice trailed off miserably as the doorbell rang again. "They said they'd meet me here."

"Oh, for the love of—" He stalked out of the door and down the steps to where she stood, hesitating. He locked his strong, warm hand around her cold wrist and yanked her toward the house. "Then you'd better get in here and explain it to them."

She followed him awkwardly, her legs stretching to keep up. There was no hope of keeping her robe shut around her thighs, but luckily he didn't seem to notice. Annoyance was palpable in the air around him. With hard fingers he pulled her through the kitchen, down the hall and into the large foyer.

"Now. Let's hear you explain this."

What a moment! The young policeman was dubious at first, but Ford turned on all his charm—and the man did have charm, she had to admit—and finally, after a long look at the Chadbourne name on the driver's license, he agreed to let it pass.

Megan shut the door with a sigh of relief. How embarrassing.

"You know what he thought, don't you?"

She looked around. Ford's voice had come from the front parlor. She moved to the doorway and watched as he found the liquor cabinet and squatted down to study the contents. In that position his back was a perfect inverted triangle, muscular shoulders tapering to a trim waist. Though the house was warm, she shivered again.

"Ah...good." He stood up, bottle in hand, and poured a rosy liquid into two brandy glasses. He turned back to her, and his green eyes were shining. "So—do you know?"

"No," she said waspishly, to hide the trembling in her voice. "What did he think?"

He came slowly toward her, a glass in each hand and a dry smile on his lips. "Well, among other things, he thought you looked dangerously sexy in that robe."

Instinctively she twisted the belt tighter, pulling the edges of the robe so that they overlapped as much as possible. "How absurd. He thought no such thing. He's a policeman."

Ford laughed and pushed the brandy toward her. "I think the operative part of that word is *man*." When she didn't lift her hand, he nudged her shoulder with the glass. "Here, take this. You need something to warm you up."

She took it reluctantly. She *was* cold. She couldn't seem to still the shaking in her legs.

"Don't judge everyone by your own standards," she said, her lips curling disdainfully. "I'm sure he understood that I was concerned. You don't check your wardrobe at times like that.''

His ironic gaze slid down her body, from her flushed cheeks to her bare feet. "Oh, come on, Meggie. Are you really such an innocent that you'd go out stalking burglars in that getup?"

The comment was unanswerable. It had been stupid.

But he didn't wait for an answer. Setting his glass down on an end table, he strode fluidly, purposefully, toward her. Before she could react, he had swept her into his hard arms.

"I'm not a criminal of any sort," he muttered, low and harsh, "and look what it does to me."

One hand pressed the small of her back so that she was molded against his muscled body. The other wrapped under her hair, behind her neck, paralyzing her face in an uptilted position. As he lowered his dark face over hers, she could smell the sharp sweetness of the brandy on his breath.

"Ford, this is—"

Her voice broke off as the perfume of his breath filled her nostrils, as incapacitating as ether. And then she could only watch helplessly as, with one smooth descent, his lips met hers.

The kiss, like the alcohol, caused a fierce burning, and she could not resist its swift, hot demands. She clung to the glass she still held, as though it could anchor her to reality, but her body was melting from the inside out, and she had to hold on to Ford to keep from falling.

It was, more than anything, a kiss of possession. It didn't coax. It didn't seduce. It merely took. His tongue invaded the softness between her teeth, as though to prove she could hold nothing back. And she could not.

She felt herself glowing white-hot under his hands, a coal being consumed by fire.

Even when he must have felt her capitulation, he didn't cease his plunder. She was his. She could not resist, could not think, could not even breathe unless he willed it.

And then he let go of her. She stumbled back, suddenly hollow, like the ashy shell of the consumed coal. He downed the rest of his brandy in one long swallow, but even when he lowered his head and looked at her again, she could see no signs of turmoil in him. His breathing was regular, his face relaxed.

The contrast with her own disorientation was humiliating. She fought the urge to slap the aloof expression from his features and struggled to compose herself.

All kinds of clichés sprang to her lips. But there was something in the ironic detachment of his expression that made phrases like "How dare you?" seem ridiculous. The kiss didn't appear to have been very significant to him, so she wouldn't flatter his impossible ego by implying it had been so to her.

"More brandy?" He held up his empty glass questioningly and turned toward the parlor, where the bottle sat on the bar. "Thank god Natalie had good taste in liquor, at least."

The disdain in his voice stung her into speech. Perhaps she couldn't berate him for kissing her, but she could safely channel some of that anger into this topic.

"She had good taste in a great many things. And why do you persist in calling your mother Natalie?"

He laughed and tossed back a huge gulp of the liquor. "What should I call her—Mommy?" His eyes roamed the room, passing over the rose damask curtains, the Victorian love seat, the curio cabinet, all with the same blank indifference he might have given an empty warehouse.

"I was ten years old when she left." He slid one hand into the pocket of his jeans and leaned back against the bar. "She was no more my mother than my father's housekeeper Bridget was. In fact, it could be argued that Bridget was a good bit more qualified for the title. At least she was *there*."

The words could have been plaintive, but somehow they weren't. She would have liked to believe he was covering a valley of pain with a mountain of indifference, but she couldn't.

"It must be nice," she retorted sarcastically, "to be so perfect that you can afford to judge everyone else so harshly."

He chuckled—not a pleasant sound. "And it must be nice," he countered, "to be so naive that you believe anything you're told."

Naive? She drew her high brows together in irritation. She had lived through too many hard times, too many crushing disappointments . . .

But he wasn't interested in that. She drew herself up.

"You never answered me. What *are* you doing here? Clearly you weren't just yearning to see your dear mother's home."

He put his glass down and gave the beautiful room another thorough scrutiny before answering. "You know, you just might be wrong about that. I *did* come to see the house. I hear that Garden District property is quite valuable these days. I have to decide what to do with the place. I might sell it." He looked thoughtful. "Or I might keep it. Especially since there's a tenant out back to offset the upkeep."

She blushed. Natalie had rented the carriage house to her for a nominal amount. Perhaps Ford felt that wasn't enough.

"If you're implying that I should pay more rent, I certain—"

"Oh, god, don't be so skittish." He interrupted her, the bored tone back in his voice. "Didn't you ever hear that the guilty flee where no man pursueth? I said nothing of the sort."

And, of course, he hadn't. She was too edgy. She couldn't relax, couldn't uncoil this disturbing knot of lingering desire. And it was hard to summon dignity in this idiotic outfit.

"Well, I'd better get back to my apartment," she said, sidestepping toward the hall. "I have a—"

She stopped in her tracks, looking, as he did, at the front door. Someone was pounding on it, so hard they could feel the vibrations under their feet.

"Megan. Megan! Are you in there?" It was Harry.

"Oh, no!" She hurried toward the door and flung it open. "Harry, I'm sorry," she said, falling over her words in her embarrassment. "I came over to see Ford— that is, I saw the lights here and I wondered—"

Harry stepped in, squinting, clearly shocked to find her there in her robe. A chill that did not come from the open door settled on the room.

"Harry Evans, this is Ford Chadbourne," she said quickly, recognizing the flash that shot between blue eyes and green. "Natalie's son. She left him the house and the business, remember?"

"No," Harry said slowly. "What *I* remember is that this is the guy from the New Year's Eve party. Only then his name was something else, or so Becky told me."

Megan groaned inwardly. She'd forgotten Harry had seen Ford before. God, what a mess. "Well, Becky was mistaken, Harry. This is Ford Chadbourne. Ford, this is Harry Evans. He owns Baubles, a jewelry store on our block."

The two men shook hands, but the veneer of civility was so thin she could see cracks in it already. Harry's face was red with annoyance, and she knew it was justified. No man would like finding his date with another man, flustered and half-undressed.

Ford, on the other hand, seemed to find the situation hugely amusing. "How about a brandy, Harry? Natalie—my *mother*, that is—really knew her brandy."

Harry was declining with forced good humor. "Thanks, but no. Megan and I have reservations for eight at Arnaud's."

"Really?" Ford's voice was polite, but the gleam in his eyes was devilish as he scanned down her robe. "Did you tell *her*?"

That was enough. "Yes, he told me," Megan jumped in, furious. "I'm sorry, Harry," she added with super sweetness in her voice. "Come on back to the carriage house, and I'll change in a jiffy. We shouldn't be more than a few minutes late."

She should have known better than to be so sugary with Harry. His ego salved, he became again the Hands-on Harry Becky liked to call him. His eyes lit up, and he grinned at Ford.

"Whoa! Maybe I'd better wait here and take that brandy." He chucked Megan's chin with his hand. "If I went with you, we might be more than a few minutes late!"

Megan held her chin still, but she wanted to scream. This was pure Harry—fatuous, infuriating, insinuating, but pure Harry. Anyone who knew him would realize it didn't mean a thing.

But Ford's eyes slid from Harry to Megan and back again, and a small blue vein pulsed in his left temple.

"Go on with her, Harry," he said evenly. "I don't give a damn whether you two *ever* get to dinner. Just make sure you get her home early. She's got a tough day at the store tomorrow."

Megan frowned. "I'm not working tomorrow. Becky is."

Ford started toward the parlor, clearly dismissing them.

"I don't know who Becky is, but *you're* going to be there tomorrow," he said coldly. "I'm coming in and I want the VIP tour. I want to see every widget in the place."

CHAPTER SIX

BY NINE O'CLOCK the next morning every piece of clothing she owned was scattered around her room. Folding her arms across her silky white slip, she surveyed the foaming sea of colors and textures with disgust. How absurd to let herself get into such a lather—she wasn't a teenager getting ready for her senior prom. What difference did it make what she wore to work today? Ford would either like Memory Lane or he wouldn't. She bit her lower lip and sighed. To be more precise, he probably wouldn't.

But already she had made one nervous change after another, until she was left with this seething heap of silks and cottons, reds and blues and greens. And a throbbing headache.

Oh, to heck with it! She grabbed the first thing her hand reached and put it on. There—she looked fine. Actually it was a pretty good compromise: a plum Shetland wool cardigan jacket over a pleated plaid wool skirt, and a white linen blouse with lacy jabot and cuffs to soften the look. She ran a brush hard through her dark curls, until they sprang full and soft from her head and her scalp tingled. Then she pinned them back loosely with a black bow.

Hoping the noise wouldn't rouse Ford, she started Natalie's Subaru gingerly and eased out of the driveway. Let him get to Memory Lane on his own. She hadn't noticed the rental Ferrari last night, and there was no sign of one now. Too bad. Let him take a taxi, like the plebeians. She bit her lip—that was too petty.

But that wasn't all. She wanted to get there first, to warn Becky and to spruce the place up a little. The card files might need straightening.

It had finally stopped raining. Enjoying the relative quiet of the as-yet-unopened Square, she walked the few blocks from her parking lot to the store, her spirits lifting with every step. She was eager to get to the store, which was for just a few more minutes her own private haven.

For five years it had served that purpose. And now Ford Chadbourne would enter it and take that away from her. She gritted her teeth, hating it. Oh, Natalie, she sighed inwardly. Why did you have to set it up this way?

As she unlocked the door, she caught her breath in a long, dizzying moment of concentrated dismay. Even from outside, through the window, she could see him. Her haven had already been violated. Ford was already there.

How dare he? He must have let himself in some time ago. He was comfortably ensconced at Natalie's beautiful desk, reading a book and acting for all the world as though he . . . as though he . . .

As though he owned the place? Finally the vise of tension relaxed. Her natural sense of the ridiculous took over and she had to smile at her own indignant sputterings. That was exactly what he *did* do. He owned the place.

"Good morning," she said cheerily, shutting the door quietly behind her and flipping the window sign to Open. She crossed the store slowly, straightening an album here, fluffing a pillow there. "You're up bright and early, aren't you? How long have you been here?"

"A while," he answered amiably, dropping the book and locking his hands behind his head. He let his eyes roam across her, from the lace at her throat to the black pumps on her feet. She returned the gaze, realizing with some irritation that he hadn't considered this a dress-up occasion. But however casually chosen, his clothes became him. Black jeans made his slim, tightly muscled hips and legs seem even tighter, and a thick turquoise and teal sweater made his broad shoulders look strong enough to—with effort she pulled her thoughts back to what he was saying.

"I always get an early start," he said. His voice was still casual but it held in its mellow depths a peculiar note that made her uneasy. "But then *I* wasn't out carousing until one in the morning, so it was no hardship."

Ahh. Good. He had noticed. She smiled brightly. She'd shocked Harry last night by insisting that they go dancing after dinner, just so that this arrogant man wouldn't have the satisfaction of thinking he had spoiled her date.

"You must have had a little trouble sleeping, though," she said politely, "or you wouldn't have known what time I got in. Couldn't you find a bed that suited you?"

"Oh, no," he insisted, equally polite. "I took the big bedroom at the back. It was quite comfortable. I rummaged around a bit and found some interesting books. I was still reading when your friend deposited you at your door."

Her determined good humor vanished as a knife-stab of resentment thrust through her. The big back room had been Natalie's. Natalie had lain for months, mortally ill, in that bed, wanting to see her son but knowing it wasn't possible. And now, now that she was gone, he dared to sleep in her lovely room, to "rummage" through her things? She had to bite her lip to keep from saying something she would regret.

Coming around the desk, she slid her purse under it, avoiding his long legs. "Well, good, then. I'm glad." Her throat was stiff, and she hoped it didn't alter her voice. "Shall we get on with it? What did you want to see first? The books and postcards together make up about sixty percent of our business, so they're really the most important. I can show you the figures."

"I've seen the figures." He sounded bored. "Now I want to see the real thing. Come on, Meggie. Show me why all these scraps of paper mean so damn much to you."

He stood up, pushing back the Queen Anne chair, which, she realized as she watched him unfold his lean length, must have been far too small for him. It had fit Natalie's tiny frame perfectly, she remembered, so Ford must have inherited his height from his father.

His father. Natalie's husband. For the first time, Megan wondered why Natalie had had to run away from her New York home. If Ford's father had been like him, if he had been as dynamic and virile as this man standing before her now, it didn't seem possible that Natalie had not loved him.

But perhaps Natalie's wisdom had been greater than hers. Natalie had known that animal magnetism and sexual chemistry alone could not make a relationship work. Unconsciously Megan backed away a couple of steps. If a man was cold and hard, it didn't matter how perfect the symmetry of his muscular body was. Smart lady. Megan was still trying to teach herself that lesson.

And Ford certainly wasn't helping. He had followed her backward movements and now stood only inches away. The fresh scent of his after-shave filled her nostrils. She hadn't ever consciously noticed it before, and yet he must have been wearing it that night—the night when he'd almost become her lover—for the smell of it now triggered a barrage of memories. She reached a shaking hand out to brace herself on the nearest armchair.

Confused, she looked into his eyes, which were suddenly smoldering. Hunter green. And she was the hunted.

She saw it quite clearly now. He was still pursuing. He still wanted her—perhaps perversely wanted her even more now that she had proved difficult to obtain. Men, spoiled, shallow men, were like that. She had seen it before.

But though she saw it clearly, she was helpless to stop the desire that swept like silent, dangerous currents between them. She leaned back slightly, as though pulling against the undertow.

"Meggie," he began, and she knew he wasn't going to talk about business. She shook her head mutely, trying to stop him from speaking. "Meggie, we—"

The chimes behind them tinkled as the door opened, and she spun quickly around. The sound might have been a magic cue that released her from his spell.

"We're closed," he called out harshly and placed a restraining hand on her shoulder. "The store opens at ten."

Clearly confused, the customer kept hold of the doorknob and pointed to the Open sign in the window. "But this—"

Her mind clearing, Megan frowned at Ford and furiously shook off his hot hand before moving with a stiff smile toward the hesitating woman.

"No, no," she assured her. "We're not closed. Please come in. Browse all you like, and if you need some help, just let me know."

Glancing dubiously at Ford, the woman nodded and made a beeline for the bookstacks. Probably just another *Gone With The Wind* fan, Megan told herself dismally, remembering that she had forgotten to bring Mr. Toby's copy in. But even so, how dare Ford Chadbourne think he had the right to turn away her customers?

"It's only a quarter to ten, you know," Ford said quietly, watching Megan from under dark brows as she scraped the chair out and planted herself behind the desk. Her movements were jerky with repressed anger. That's all, she assured herself. Anger, pure and simple. The rest of it, the waves of awareness, the currents of desire, were mere phantoms. The real battle between them was not over kisses and longing. It was over dollars and cents.

Too furious to speak she pulled out a receipt book before answering and scribbled today's date on it. January twenty-five. The significance didn't escape her—as of today, she had only one month in which to win this wretched bet. And he would just love to distract her, wouldn't he? To cloud her judgment, to tie her psyche in knots with his husky voice and his unwelcome kisses.

In her anger she pressed the pen so hard she almost tore the paper. Finally she looked up, her gray eyes blazing.

"Until midnight on Mardi Gras, Memory Lane opens early and closes late." With difficulty she kept her steel-edged voice low. "And you keep your distance. I can't keep you out of here, but I want you to know that I see what you're up to. You think you can rattle me, don't you? That's what you came down here for—to make sure I lose."

She lowered her voice to a hot hiss as the customer wandered closer. "Well, go right ahead. Try whatever you like. Wear the most sensual after-shave you can find. Stand too close, and use your best bedroom voice. You can move in next door or camp out here in the armchair. Those cheap tricks won't get you anywhere. And do you know why? Because you *don't* rattle me any more, Ford. I understand you too well."

She pointed her flashing silver pen at him and narrowed her gray eyes to furious slits. "But *you* understand this. I don't care if it's 6:00 a.m. or midnight. Don't you ever, ever turn a customer away again, or the deal's off."

She was too angry to regret her words, but she met his gaze defiantly, the white lace at her throat quivering as she breathed raggedly. Would there be retribution for her insulting words? She remembered the mousy Jim Brackett, who obviously feared the Chadbourne wrath.

To her shock the smooth skin around his eyes crinkled, a movement too small to be a smile but clearly not the precursor of wrath. He settled himself on the edge of the desk, his long thigh only inches away from her trembling hands.

"What a passionate young woman you are, Meggie Farrell," he said mildly, his eyes straying over her face. She frowned, realizing by the heat under her eyes that she must be flaming with indignation. She knew all too well how she looked, fine nostrils flaring, eyes flashing. Damn her treacherous face.

He chuckled. "Oh, you hate that, don't you? You don't want anyone to know. You like to pretend you're all ice, all business, all control." He reached out and brushed his hand across her rigid fingers, which gripped the cool pen so hard her knuckles were stretched white.

"But I know better, don't I? I knew you before you were on your guard, before you threw all your defenses up."

She restrained the urge to pull her hand away. How proud he was of his little charade. Why flatter him further by letting him know his touch could still disturb her?

"Is that why you were here before, Ford?" she asked coldly, holding her hand as still as if it were made of wax. "A little reconnoitering? A quick foray into enemy territory, under an assumed name, of course?"

His eyes narrowed, and his words came harshly. "Well, you can't blame me for being curious, can you? After twenty years of silence Natalie suddenly remembers her long-lost son...and suddenly I inherit a business I'd never even heard of *and* its loyal young employee, one Megan Farrell, who for all I knew had been expecting to inherit the store herself." He gazed around him at the store, apparently unaware that his hand still rested on hers, burning into her skin. "Frankly I don't think it's so surprising that I should have wanted to see for myself what my mother and this Megan Farrell had been up to. Do you?"

"No," she admitted honestly. "Not at first. But later, after we met...later when we..." She blushed, furious with herself for the plaintive note that had slipped into her voice.

He heard it, too, and his grip tightened. "Later what? You think I should have told you who I really was? But I couldn't, could I?" His eyes held hers as his hand massaged the back of her fist, pushing currents of electric awareness past the barriers of rigid muscles, up her arm and into her body.

"No, Meggie, by then it was too late. You see, I had already discovered that passion you're trying so hard to hide right now...and I had to go on being Tony Ford. I don't think you'd have opened your door for Ford Chadbourne that night, would you?''

Would she? She remembered the need that had pulsated through her, drowning the doubts that had tried to surface. He could have told her almost anything that night, and she still would have let him in. Almost anything—anything except the truth.

As she tried to formulate an answer through her frozen lips, the chimes rang again, and Becky breezed in.

'''Morning, all!'' she called, eyeing Ford with interest.

Relieved, Megan pulled her hand away, grateful that Ford didn't try to stop her.

But he didn't rise from his perch on the edge of the desk.

"Saved by the bell," he said. "But remember—you're not fooling anybody with this icy act, Meggie. Except maybe yourself.''

"WELL, IF YOU DON'T want him, honey, *I* do.''

It was a week later, and Becky was lounging in Megan's living room, a glass of white wine half-forgotten on the table at her elbow. They were supposed to be working, but instead Becky was staring shamelessly out the window, waiting for a light to go on in Natalie's house.

She seemed destined for disappointment—it was almost eleven o'clock, and the garden was still dark. There was no sign of Ford. Megan refused to let her own eyes stray to the window, but she couldn't help wondering where he was. Where *could* he be, so late at night? Did he know other people in New Orleans? Or was he back at the French Quarter, looking for someone else, someone as lonely and vulnerable as she had been that Christmas Eve . . . was it really only six weeks ago?

"Want Ford Chadbourne? No, you don't, Becky," she said firmly as she pulled a new stack of postcards out of the box at her feet. Her shoulders ached, and her eyes were blurry from hours of pricing, but she'd just bought two thousand cards, an entire estate, and she wanted to get them into stock before the weekend. "You may be the most sophisticated Southern belle in this burg, but he plays in another league. He has little blondes like you for breakfast."

"Hmm." Becky lay across the sofa and inspected her pink nails for any sign of chipping. Her voice registered frank incredulity. "I bet he hasn't ever met any little blondes like me before."

Laughing, Megan shook her head and priced another card. "Don't kid yourself. In fact, he has a little blonde of his very own. I met her. The daughter of his late partner. Named Krista Kelly. She worships him."

"Well, of course she does, honey. Men like that take worship for granted. But the important question is, does *he* worship *her*?"

Megan stared at the postcard in front of her, not really seeing it, seeing instead the soft glances Ford had bestowed on Krista. Unfailingly, they had been protective, gentle ... so different from the flashing gaze he so often turned on her. The tender way he had kissed Krista's brow, the care he took never to disagree with her ...

"I think he may," she heard herself saying in a benumbed voice. Did he? Did he love the gentle Krista, did he have plans to marry her, even while he lusted after the red-lipped nobody from New Orleans? "I think he may," she repeated dully.

Dismayed, she closed her eyes. How horrible to be so jealous! She'd never felt jealousy before, never known that it gnawed at your stomach until you felt sick. And yet here she was, cruelly jealous. Even though she despised him, she couldn't seem to forget the way his hands had felt on her skin, the way his lips had pulled her into a storm of raw passion. And even worse, she couldn't forget the way she had gloried in the turbulence of that storm; the power, the feelings that whipped her into a whirlwind of ecstasy.

Oh, god, he had been right. She was only fooling herself with this facade of detached serenity. Inside, Megan Farrell churned with passion for her work, for all beauty, and now that she had stood at the edge of the storm and felt its power, for love. Something inside her ached like a hunger for more. More passion. Another storm.

"Well, shoot!" Becky folded her hands over her lap, looking disgusted. "Why didn't you tell me he was already taken? I've spent this entire week drooling on his shoes like a lonely lapdog. And here we've wasted a perfectly good Saturday night waiting around for him to bring his sexy body on home. He probably took it up to New York for the weekend."

Megan opened her eyes, amused in spite of her tension by Becky's theatrics. "I'm wounded," she teased. "I thought you said you wanted to help me price postcards."

"Well, I do, I do." Becky sat up and scooped up a handful of cards. "Especially now. Now we've *got* to beat this guy. If I'd known he had a honey in New York, I'd have been a little more enthusiastic about winning this dumb bet."

"Then I'm glad I told you," Megan said grimly. "I could use a little enthusiasm. We're way behind schedule. It's going to take a miracle to pull this one off."

"How much do you still have to come up with?"

"Six thousand." Megan spoke the words between clenched teeth. Only three weeks, less than half the allotted time, to make more than half the agreed profit. Depression threatened to engulf her. She had been working so hard. She'd left no stone unturned. She'd twirled her Rolodex, calling former customers to tell them about new merchandise, until her fingers were sore. She had stayed open hours after everything else on the street was closed, hoping for a bored tourist coming home from Bourbon Street with a few dollars in his pocket. She'd even broken up the set of Dickens novels, something Natalie would never have considered, when a customer wanted only one title. She had reassured doubtful customers, coaxed reluctant ones, babied lazy ones. She had done everything but go door-to-door.

"Oh, lord!" Becky sounded horrified. "Six thousand? Shoot, we might as well give up, honey. That's too much."

"No, it's not." Megan forced confidence into her voice. "Only one more week until the Mardi Gras season heats up. Those two weeks before Mardi Gras, when there are parades almost every day, are the biggest weeks of our year. Natalie's been known to clear two thousand a week during a good Mardi Gras."

Becky shook her head. "Can't you add, kiddo? That's four thousand. Not six."

"Well, I'll do something special. I'll..." She cast frantically for inspiration, just as she had done every day, every night, for the past five weeks. And as usual, she slammed into a painful blank wall of frustration. "I don't know. I just know I'll do it."

"But how?" Becky held up the postcards she had been pricing. "Either they want this stuff or they don't. You know how it is. Half the people who come in don't have the faintest idea what Memory Lane is all about. You couldn't even sell that three-hanky Civil War diary to some of them. They'd just think it was too old and yellow. They couldn't imagine what they'd use it for."

"I know, I know," Megan agreed unhappily. "And yet there are so many ways... if only they'd use a little imagination...."

"Some of these people don't *have* any imagination," Becky grumbled, bending over her cards. "So it's no use asking them to use any."

Megan stared at her. Something was stirring inside her, something that felt miraculously like hope. That was it! That was the "something special" she could do. She could *show* customers how to use these things. She had enough imagination to go around! The hope lurched inside her, and laughter bubbled out.

"That's it!" Jumping up, she hugged Becky, who looked dumbstruck.

"It is?"

"Yes, yes, yes!" Megan sat on the sofa beside her and talked rapidly. "We'll *show* them what Memory Lane's merchandise can be used for. Not the diary—that'll probably sell to some museum or library, and researching and authenticating it will take too long to help us here. But the other stuff, the stuff they don't understand. We'll take a theme—let's say children. We'll take an old-fashioned christening dress, a postcard of a little Victorian girl, a charming old children's book, and frame them together. Or high school—everybody feels nostalgic about their high school. We'll take an old high school diploma, a postcard of the school as it looked way back when, a car ad picturing the car they drove to Lover's Lane in..."

Her eyes were bright with excitement. "Oh, it'll be such fun, Becky! And we can take occupations. Lawyers, doctors, dentists, architects, teachers. And for each one, we'll frame a collage of appropriate pictures, maps, books, illustrations—anything. We can even make collections to order. There has to be a fortune out there in orders from interior decorators." She laughed delightedly. "We'll just tap into it, that's all."

Becky still looked skeptical. "In three weeks?"

"I know—it sounds crazy, but we can do it. Let's have an open house. We'll get samples made, and we'll invite everyone to a showing, just like the galleries do. All the professional people who have offices to decorate, all the interior designers, all the restaurateurs—we'll invite everybody in this town who has a wall to hang a picture on!"

"But..." Becky looked almost frightened by Megan's fervor. "You'd have to work twenty-four hours a day to pull this off. And the orders might not even start coming in until it's too late."

"I'm not afraid of work." Megan wouldn't be dissuaded. This had the right feel. She just knew it would work. She could almost imagine Natalie smiling. "And even one big commission could put us over the top. Let's do it, Becky. Let's do it."

She poured out fresh glasses of wine for both of them.

"Come on, Becky, smile. It may be the craziest thing I've ever done, but it just might work." They clinked glasses in a toast, Becky still shaking her head incredulously. Megan drank the cool liquid in one long swallow, though she didn't taste a drop.

Her head reeled suddenly, though whether it was from the wine or from the excitement she couldn't be sure. Dimly she realized she probably shouldn't have had two glasses—she had worked through dinner, and her stomach was empty. But it didn't matter. Finally there was hope, and she was drunk with that as much as with the wine.

When the telephone rang, she answered it gaily. She stood at the window, excitedly hugging her stomach with one hand and the receiver with the other. In her preoccupation she didn't realize she was looking out at golden rectangles of light where earlier there had been darkness, until she heard Ford's deep voice in her ear.

"Do you have company?"

Stunned and still reeling, she didn't answer at first. So he hadn't gone to New York. He was here.

"Megan?" His voice deepened. "Do you have company?"

"Yes." She didn't elaborate. She didn't trust her voice. Even the electronic transmission of his voice seemed to pierce her ear, streaking like a hot hairline of lightning down into the pit of her stomach.

"Who is it?" His voice was gruff now but no less potent on her nerves.

"Becky. We're working." She sounded like an automaton.

"Well, can you wind it up now? I need to see you."

He did? "Why?"

He made a sound that could have been exasperation. "I'll tell you when you get here. Just wind it up."

CHAPTER SEVEN

FORD HAD flicked on the yard lights, but she didn't need them. A thousand stars lit her way across the garden. Pausing by an iron bench that glowed milky white in the starlight, she stared up at the big house.

A thrill shivered through her as a cold breeze lifted her hair and blew across the sensitive pulse just under her jaw. She ought to go in. She hadn't bothered to grab a coat, and though she wore a long black sweater over her black jeans, already the air was sliding cold fingers inside the wool and raising goose bumps on her skin.

Climbing the short flight of stairs to the porch, she knocked lightly at the kitchen door. He answered so quickly she wondered if he had been standing at the window, watching her.

"Thank you for coming." His voice was almost expressionless.

She raised one brow. "You're welcome," she said politely, although the exchange surprised her. She'd really had no choice—he *was* the boss. "What's up? It sounded important."

He shrugged, shifting his broad shoulders under the yellow lambswool of his sweater. "In here," he said, leading the way toward the library. "I want to talk."

She followed, trying not to be aware of the grace of his body as he walked in front of her. It was a thing of beauty, truly, with its classic lines and its rippling strength, but surely she could just admire it in the same impersonal way she admired a Greek statue, or Michelangelo's *David*. She didn't have to think about how warm his flesh would be under her fingers or how the arms could close around her, shutting out the world.

She rubbed her palms nervously on her thighs, trying to work strength back into them. Already they were trembling, and though she told herself it was just the shock of going from the frost outside to the warmth inside, in her heart she knew better.

The library was the only room in the house that wasn't ornate with Victorian furniture. She had always thought of it as a man's room, and never more so than now. The built-in mahogany bookshelves, the oversized armchairs, the leather sofa, everything was bathed in a golden light from a leaping fire.

He belonged in this room, she thought as she watched him stoke the fire. The brass poker glinted, as the stirred up bittersweet scent of burning pine wafted toward her sensitive nostrils, mingling along the way with a tantalizing trace of his after-shave.

She couldn't take her eyes from him. As he bent over the logs, the strong bones of his face were both accentuated and softened by the honeyed shadows. A lock of his mahogany hair had fallen forward onto his broad forehead and burned red gold in the firelight. Her fingers twitched with the urge to smooth it back into place, and she curled them into fists.

The log he touched fell easily into the arms of the fire, releasing a shower of white-hot sparks as it met the tongues of flame. Silently he watched until the sparks had settled in the ashes, then slowly he sheathed the poker and turned to her.

As their eyes met, her heart lurched, panicked, in her breast. Oh, no. She should run, as fast as her melting legs would carry her. She should flee into the sensible, bracing night air, away from the smothering intimacy of this hot room. It would be beyond her power to resist him in this room, where his eyes were more golden than green, like a forest on fire. Not here, where the fire drew them down into a hot bath of sensuality.

"Sit down," he said, and she mindlessly obeyed, dropping onto the sofa. The leather molded itself around her contours, as though it would hold her there forever, a soft but mighty prison. She heard the clink of a bottle against crystal, the trickle of liquid falling from a narrow spout, and knew she ought to protest. She'd had enough to drink.

But she took the tawny wineglass without a word and sipped gratefully from its cool rim. It didn't matter whether she drank one glass or twenty. She had been powerless ever since she entered this room. Or maybe it had been long before that.

He didn't sit beside her, didn't try to press his advantage, though he must have known he could. Instead he stood in front of her, one elbow hooked over the dark wood mantelpiece, his wineglass dangling over the fire. In that position it seemed lit from within, like some wizard's magic potion. But he didn't drink it. She studied his face with a twinge of surprise. He didn't look like a man bent on seduction. Strain had etched tired lines around his mouth, and his eyes were hollowed and shadowy. He looked—he looked sad. Or was it just a trick of the firelight?

"I want you to tell me about my mother," he said suddenly.

Her brow furrowed, and she tilted her head, looking closer into his face. But it was hard to read, the firelight shifted so. "What do you mean?"

"Just tell me," he repeated, still staring into the orange flames. "Tell me what she was like when you knew her."

"Well, she was..." Megan hesitated, searching for the right words. Natalie had been so many things. "Strong— she was very strong, very brave. Proud. A little difficult to live with. She had very definite opinions about things." She couldn't tell whether this was what he wanted to know. "But she was very wise. I depended on her more than she realized."

Finally he looked at her, but the turning of his face away from the fire threw it into shadows, and she could see only the outline of his cheek and his jaw.

"Was she happy?"

Megan bit her lip. That was a difficult question. "Not exactly," she said carefully. "Her wisdom seemed to come from experience, you see, experience with the harder side of life." She hated having to say these things. Somehow, tonight, she didn't want to say things that would hurt him. "Why are you asking all these questions? Why tonight?"

At first he didn't answer. Turning back to the fire, he stared into it, as though he'd lost something there. When he finally spoke, his voice was dull. "I found some postcards in her room today."

That didn't surprise her. This old house was full of postcards. Natalie had been a collector as well as a retailer. But his tone implied more, so she waited for him to explain.

"There must have been a hundred of them," he continued. "And they were all addressed to me."

Megan gasped as she began to understand. She hadn't known about the cards—Natalie had never shown them to her. And yet, knowing Natalie, suddenly their existence made perfect sense. Natalie had always said that Memory Lane was the caretaker of the past. "This isn't just merchandise, Meggie," she had said vehemently. "This is people. It is all that's left of their love for one another."

How fitting that, during all those years, she'd been writing down her feelings for the son she'd had to abandon. Was that why she had willed the house and the business to him—so that he could come here someday and find the love she had kept carefully tied up in ribbons?

Sensing his confusion, Megan reached out to him, but he had his back to her, his mind still probing the secrets of the fire. She dropped her hand, unseen, into her lap.

"The first one was written twenty years ago, the day she left New York." His voice was emotionless, but his posture was rigid, his back stiff and his arms tensed. "The last was written just before she died. And all the years between. Christmas, my birthday—"

He whirled around abruptly, and Megan drew in a hard breath. "Damn it!" he exploded. "Why didn't she mail them? Even *one* of them? All those years..."

Without thinking, she stood up, dropped her wineglass on the end table and rushed to him. Her heart was aching, not just for the plaintive echo of the boy she heard behind Ford's angry words, but for Natalie as well.

"I think maybe she was too hurt, Ford," she said, laying her hand over his stiff, muscular one. She wished she could draw the pain out of him and into herself, the way you might draw poison from a wound. "She found it very difficult to ask for anything."

If he noticed her touch he didn't show it. His eyes were curiously unfocused, as though they looked far beyond her, into the past. "She said, on one of the cards, that my father hated her. That she had been afraid he would grow to hate me, too, if she stayed. As though any reason could justify what she did!"

"But perhaps she was right," Megan cut in, eager to support Natalie. Ford, who had been only a child when his mother ran away, hadn't known Natalie as Megan had, hadn't known what an unflinchingly honest person she was. If she wrote that on the postcard, then she had sincerely believed it. Natalie didn't lie. "She knew your father, probably saw him even more objectively than you did. She may have been right."

Megan reached out and touched his hand. "But even if she was wrong, she meant well, Ford. I know she did. She loved you."

Finally he looked up at her with burning eyes.

"Loved me? She never even knew me!" Megan murmured a denial, but he ignored it, his resentment clearly ran too strong to be quelled by her gentle voice. "You're a passionate woman, Megan. Is that the way you'd show love for a son of yours?"

As his words sank in, dropping like rocks into the pit of her stomach, her eyes fluttered shut, as if to avoid facing the truth of his words. In her mind's eye she saw herself a mother. Could she ever leave her son behind? A son of her blood, who might have his father's green eyes, her own black curls... Could she leave their child as Natalie had left Ford—or as Patrick Kelly had left her?

"No!" she cried, opening her eyes, unable to bear the vision any longer. "No, never." Hot tears formed behind her lids, not falling, but blurring his image. "But that isn't fair. Everyone is different. Every situation is different. She must have been terribly unhappy. There were things you and your father did—"

He grabbed her shoulders. "*I* was only ten years old, Megan. What could I have done?"

She shook her head miserably.

"I don't know—" she struggled. "I just don't know. Maybe it was just your father. And she must have believed it would be harder for you if she had stayed."

"But I didn't have a chance to find out, did I?" Though his voice was cold, his hands on her shoulders were hot.

Looking into his hard eyes, she realized she must have been mad to imagine this man could be vulnerable. There was no pain in him, only a cold, enduring anger.

"Did I?" He repeated the question persistently, his fingers digging deeper into her flesh.

"I don't know," she ground out between clenched teeth, the pain in her shoulders almost equalling the pain in her heart.

The whole thing was tearing her apart. Back before Natalie died, before she ever met Ford, she had thought it was all so tragically simple—the good woman versus the heartless monsters. Now everything was turned upside down. And yet, heartbreakingly, it was just as tragic. Everyone was to blame. And at the same time, perhaps no one was. Poor Natalie. Poor Ford. Poor little Meggie. Love was such a dangerous game.

"I can't explain her, can't defend her," she said, her ragged voice dropping to a near whisper. "I don't know the answers any more than you do. I can only tell you what you ought to know already—that no one is ever completely right, and no one is ever completely wrong. The world isn't that easy, Ford. It's a terrifying, treacherous maze of gray."

But in spite of her conciliatory words, his cruel grip never relaxed, and finally all the pain that was tormenting her, all the unfairness of this inquisition, became unendurable. Her voice was hoarse as she twisted under his hands.

"Why are you putting me through this? Do you hate your mother so much you can't bear for *anyone* to love her? Are you so bitter that you want to poison my memories of her, too? Why don't you leave me alone?" She'd meant to sound coldly furious, and was appalled to hear her voice sound thick with unshed tears.

With one last, violent wrench she tried to free herself, but his hands held. Well, he could still her body, but not her fury. She glared at him through eyes she knew were flashing.

"I said leave me alone," she repeated slowly, sharpening her words to an ice-pick point. "What do you care what I think of your mother? Just what do you *care*?"

Fire shot from his eyes, and his arms clenched with a convulsive spasm, crushing her up violently against his chest. Green eyes seemed to gouge into gray. Wool met wool in a quiet explosion, and her legs, slammed against his muscled thighs, seemed to disappear, so little use were their wobbly stalks to her. She was held up only by his punishing hands and the granite wall of his chest.

"I care," he bit back. "I care, dammit, because you care!" His glare dug into her. "You blame me with every self-righteous bone in your body. Did you think I didn't know? Do you think I don't see it in your eyes every time you look at me? You may talk nobly of a world in shades of gray, but you don't believe it yourself. You've already decided I'm the villain of this story. You hate me because my mother taught you to hate me."

"No—" she began, outraged. Natalie had never spoken of hatred. But his tidal wave of accusations drowned her voice.

"Oh, yes, you do. You didn't look at me like this, with your gray eyes spitting lightning, when you thought I was Tony Ford. Oh, no. Then your eyes were clear and open and, god, the most beautiful eyes I had ever seen. But in New York . . . they were full of scorn, because I was Ford Chadbourne. And you wonder why I didn't tell you who I was."

He dragged his hands across her collar bone and up her neck, slowly and with an intense pressure that pulled her chin high and tilted her head back toward the fire.

"But by god I'll make you see it's not that simple," he said, his head bent so low she seemed to feel the words rather than hear them. The vibrations dropped hot and moist onto her waiting lips. "I may be Ford Chadbourne, but I'm that other man, too, and you're going to have to live with that. I'm the man you most despise and the man you most desire, all in one."

Oh, yes. Oh, yes, he was. But what could she do? Her heart beat wildly, and then seemed to stop beating altogether. But his heart picked up the rhythm for her, throbbing against her breast with slow, deep strokes. She wouldn't pull away now, not now that he was breathing for her, not now that their bodies were hopelessly entwined.

"And I know all the Megans in you, too." He ran his thumbs along the underside of her jaw and brought his lips to her ear, where the words fell with a sizzling heat down into the very core of her. "I know the Megan who is afraid." He licked at the soft ridge of her ear, and she shuddered convulsively. "And I know the Megan who is on fire."

She groaned, and with a swift movement his fingers buried themselves in her tumbled hair. His hot palms cupped around her ears, shutting off all normal sounds, trapping her in a sea-shell world of roaring emptiness.

The only reality for her now was his eyes, those mesmerizing, blinding green eyes that were fixed on her lips. Her mouth fell open, as though in answer to his unspoken demand.

It was a kiss of more volcanic intensity than any she had ever imagined, his lips moving hard and deep over hers, and still it wasn't enough. By the time his mouth reached hers, she was burning with the need that had been raging behind the locked door of her heart ever since she had met him. The touch of his lips opened that door, and the pent-up fire burst free with an explosion that threatened to consume both of them.

Her hands swept up over the arms that held her and into the thick hair at the back of his neck. With shaking hands she pulled his head closer, her fingers pressing into the proudly rounded bone that lay beneath the mahogany silk. Teeth seemed to bruise against teeth, and with a groan he responded by thrusting his tongue deeper between her aching lips.

Lights flashed and spun behind her eyes as the boundaries between their bodies blurred, as she lost all sense of where her lips ended and his began, all certainty of whether she inhaled his breath or her own.

His hands slipped lower, gliding down the long curve of her back to the soft swell where her long sweater cupped around her thighs. In one swift, seasoned movement, he'd found the waistband of her slacks and was sliding them smoothly over her hips and down the numb columns of her legs.

Now bare, her legs glistened in the firelight, as though they had just been created and were still wet with the artist's paint. She moaned again as he took each leg, one at a time, into both hands, starting at the ankle and smoothing his fingers upward, across the calf, the knee, the thigh, until they disappeared into the shadows of her sweater.

But the upper half of her body was still in darkness, waiting to be brought to life. She stood as silent as a statue as he rose to his feet and reached for the black wool that covered her, pulling it slowly over her head. Tossing the sweater aside, with expert hands he released her breasts from the white lace that chafed their now-sensitive tips. They spilled, high and rounded and swollen, into the rosy glow of the firelight.

"Oh, my beautiful Meggie." His eyes devoured her, but his hands were gentle as they brushed slowly across the silken skin, circling but never touching the puckered nipples. She tried to wait, but the sensations were strangling her, and she clutched at his reaching arm, stilling it. Her hands shook, her legs shook, and finally he took pity on her weakness.

He sank to his knees, pulling her with him. And then, with hands as tender as if they had belonged to her beloved Tony Ford, he laid her back against the soft rug.

Still fully dressed himself, he knelt over her nakedness, poising himself above her, his palms holding his weight as he leaned forward. Slowly he drew a scalding line with his tongue, from the pulse at the base of her throat, down between her breasts, and beyond, to the gentle swell of her navel.

She inhaled, desperately seeking enough air to keep from fainting, and the breath was filled with smoky pine and the musky scent of him. She reached out, groping for the edge of his sweater, but he pulled away from her hand.

"Not yet," he whispered and dropped his head to her breast.

After such lingering torture of anticipation, the touch was electrifying. His lips closed around the nipple, and he pulled it slightly, just enough to make colors burst inside her head. Her head thrown back, she twisted against the rug, driven by instincts she didn't understand.

With building intensity his head moved from one breast to the other, and the room swirled around her as she arced toward him, calling out his name and digging her fingers hard into his hair. In her mind she was looking into the blue center of a flame. Everything flickered and paled around it, and she couldn't take her eyes from the throbbing, candent point of light.

When he pulled his head away and slid down, trailing molten kisses across her belly, she was lost. In a flickering instant the flame exploded, shattering reality into a thousand shards of firelight that seemed to scatter across the heavens and then spin earthward in a dizzying spiral.

Frightened, feeling herself falling, she cried out his name, and he was there, lying beside her, cradling her scorched body in his strong arms. She wept into his shoulder, and then, gradually, when her body stopped its shuddering, the pieces of her drifted back together, and she was whole again. Weak and mystified, but whole.

He stroked her damp hair back from her forehead gently. Gratefully she let his cool fingers wipe the moisture away from under her eyes, behind her hair, along the column of her neck. But almost immediately the sensation changed. She shifted restlessly, aware that each simple touch was stoking the heat that still simmered inside her. Amazingly, though her body was still weak, a new blaze was building from the cinders of the old. She murmured helplessly, as rising flames seemed to lick at her.

Stilling the murmur with a kiss, he eased from her and stood up. With dismay she saw his silhouette rise against the fire.

"No," she whispered. "Don't go. That can't be all." She lay her hand across her aching belly. "It wasn't enough."

"Oh, no, Meggie," he said softly, looking down at her with slow-burning eyes. "It was just the beginning."

She could see only his black outline against the blazing orange fire, but it was enough to set her heart thundering as he pulled his yellow sweater over his head and then bent his arms to loosen the buttons of his shirt. When he let his jeans slide down his long, muscular legs, desire twisted at her with a fearful power, and she knifed forward, grabbing her knees for support.

"Ford—you know that nothing has changed, don't you?" Suddenly frightened of the raw masculinity she could see in the bold outlines of his body, she knew she had to be honest, whatever it cost her. She only prayed it wouldn't end the way it had the last time. She didn't think she could survive it if he left her now. "I haven't—I still haven't—"

"Shhh," he whispered, kneeling again before her. Easing her arms away from her trembling knees, he nudged her legs apart to make room for his hard body to slip between. "It's all right, Meggie. You don't have to. *I* have."

Smiling raggedly into her tentative gaze, he dipped his head again to hers and wrapped his strong arms around her, pulling her up to meet the surging need of his body. Freed at last from that final fear, she pressed herself to him joyously, giving herself over to the miracle of joining.

She would never have asked him to be gentle. She even hoped he hadn't guessed her inexperience, for she was beyond caring, beyond patience, ready to meet any pain gladly. But he was too experienced not to understand. With an effort of restraint so fierce it made his face gleam with beads of perspiration, he held back, stroking into her so slowly, with such gentleness in his rock-hard body, that the inevitable stab of pain was insignificant, melting immediately into the bigger burning.

He knew the instant her low gasp of discomfort gave way to a more urgent plea for release, and with a low groan he finally unleashed his own desire. Her hands dug deeply into his sweating back, guiding him toward a fiercer tempo, a more savage force, until finally the hot springs of passion were struck, and ecstasy boiled forth in a bewildering geyser that overwhelmed them both.

Scalding tears ran in hot rivulets from her eyes as he pulled her over, to rest against the slippery, spent muscles of his chest. As she lay in his arm, her cheek wet with the mingled tears and sweat, his ragged breathing grew still, and his heart beat rhythmically under her hand.

The fire crackled quietly—it, too, was spent. But she didn't even notice the creeping cold that was threatening the room. She had taken the warmth inside her, and her whole body burned with an incandescent glow.

He cared. He must. He had protected her, in every way there was for a man to protect a woman. His body had not just taken hers, it had worshipped it. She had nothing to compare their lovemaking to, but she somehow knew it had been profoundly important. It couldn't have been just another night, not even for this man who probably had had so many nights. It *couldn't* have been.

Gradually, as his heart thumped slowly against her hand, her moist eyes grew heavy, and she slept.

HIS VOICE—it sounded far away and tender, its caressing tones falling over her like a thick, warm liquid. Murmuring contentedly, she wriggled, only a fraction of her mind even registering where she was. A profound lethargy dragged at her limbs. That soft tickle at her bare back felt like a blanket. Ford had covered her, and now he was murmuring something sweet. She tried to focus. . . .

"It's okay. Hey, it's okay." She heard words, but he sounded far away. She tried to open her eyes, but they were sealed shut, so she settled for a sleepy smile.

"Krista, honey. . . it's okay."

The smile dropped like an anchor from her lips as a sharp wind of understanding pierced her lethargy. Krista? Krista! Ford was not talking to her. Of course—that was the gentle tone he reserved for Krista Kelly. Her flesh crawling disagreeably, Megan huddled into herself, unable, unwilling to figure it out, hoping she was caught in the grip of some crazy nightmare.

She folded her arms across her bare chest and turned her face toward the carpet. Oh, god. Maybe she *was* still sleeping. Maybe she would wake in a few minutes to find him drowsing, sated and spent, beside her.

"Krista, listen." Why couldn't she will the words away? "I'll be there in fifteen minutes. No, honey, stop worrying. It's simple. You wanted to see Mardi Gras. You wanted to see me." His voice took on a teasing note. "What could be more natural? We're both irresistible, you know."

Yes, Megan cried inwardly, as the words scratched at her, leaving her raw, with nerves exposed. Yes. I know.

"Now stop that right now," he was insisting, but with no anger in his voice. He might have been talking to an adored child. "You were coming tomorrow anyhow. You're not interrupting anything, you silly little cabbage."

She wasn't? At that, Megan knew that the nightmare was real. She tossed the soft blanket back and stood up. No, of course she wasn't interrupting. Ford had already been given everything he wanted.

The room was dark, except where the moonlight streamed in through the window, but she could just make out his outline near the desk. The telephone was jammed against one crooked shoulder and his strong jaw, and he was busily tucking in his shirttails, buttoning his cuffs with rushed fingers.

He must have heard her movements, but still murmuring reassuring syllables into the phone, he didn't say a word to her as she felt for her discarded sweater and pulled it over her head. She slipped into her black pants, and balling her underclothes up into a furious handful of white, she moved toward the door.

"Krista. Don't worry. Just buy yourself a magazine and sit down and wait for me," he ordered, his voice registering impatience for the first time. "I'll be there in fifteen minutes."

She heard the brisk click of the receiver as he dropped it back into place and the sound of his footsteps coming toward her, but she kept walking.

"Hey." He grabbed her arm and swung her around into him.

She stiffened, hating the easy cascade of goose bumps his touch was pouring over her. Easy—that word was the hallmark of their entire relationship. It had been so easy for him. What a fool she was! No wonder he had wanted her here tonight. With Krista coming tomorrow, he must have felt his time was running out. And Ford Chadbourne wasn't accustomed to doing without what he wanted. A wave of shame washed over her. He hadn't needed to work very hard, had he? She had fallen right into his hands.

As if sensing her tension, he pulled back and looked into her eyes. His own eyes were glinting, but his dark hair was rumpled, damp and spiked like the hair on a sleepy little boy's head. She hardened her heart against all those things.

In spite of her internal turmoil, she stared back, raising her brows in calm query. She would not let him see her shame. A boreal frost was settling over her, and she knew her eyes were as blankly gray as a winter dawn.

"I guess you heard," he said, his voice tentative for the first time. "That was Krista. I wasn't expecting them until tomorrow, but her mother sent her early, alone. She's at the airport now."

She nodded, though her neck was almost too rigid to bend. "Yes, I heard. You'd better get going. You don't want to keep her waiting alone there at night."

"I know. Poor kid. She's not used to traveling alone." He sounded distracted, annoyed, perhaps, but hardly heartbroken. Then he let out his breath through his teeth. "Damn—I hate leaving you like this, Meggie. Will I see you later?"

"I suppose so. I'll be at the store tomorrow, as usual." She put her hand on the brass doorknob, which was as cold as marble. As cold as her heart.

"I didn't mean at the store," he said. "I meant something more . . . satisfying. I don't think tonight was quite enough, do you?"

She narrowed her eyes. "I think it'll have to be," she said, tight-lipped. "Your friend would make this sort of thing a bit awkward, don't you think?"

A muscle flinched in his jaw, but he just stood there, staring at her.

A wave of nausea rolled over her. Later, he'd said. So he had it all figured out already. Probably this had been his plan all along. She was to be the late-night lady, the one at whose door he came rapping when the ball was over and his prim and proper girlfriend had been safely taken home. Rage fought with shame, and she had to struggle to keep her voice polite.

"I'm going to be busy, anyway," she said, proud of the nonchalance in her voice. "I have a business to run and a deadline breathing down my neck. I think I'd better stick to that for a while, don't you?"

"Well, I'm not feeling very practical right now." There was no evading him when he reached for her. With his whole body he pressed her against the door, and he slid hard hands up under her sweater. Cupping her cold breasts, he rubbed his fingers over the nipples with a possessive confidence.

"You may refuse to acknowledge it," he muttered, nipping at her lips between words, "but tonight was wonderful. You are wonderful. I could make love to you forever."

His fingers were shooting small jets of flame into her body, and she twisted away desperately, groping for the doorknob. Finding it, she pulled. Raw, pinching air rushed in.

"That's great," she said as lightly as she could. She turned her face to the frosty night, letting the wind blow across her, freezing out the flames—freezing out all feeling, leaving her benumbed, glaciated.

He frowned dangerously as she slipped through the doorway. "I said it was wonderful, Meggie," he repeated slowly, as though she had not heard him. "I meant it."

He sounded almost angry, as if miffed at her indifference. So he wanted compliments, she thought with a bitter internal laugh, on top of everything else. He wanted to be told he had made the moon rock, the earth tremble. Well, he'd have to be satisfied with what he had already been given. It was all she had.

"Oh, for me, too," she called in an elaborately casual voice as she tripped hastily down the steps on feet she couldn't feel. "It was very nice, actually. Well, see you at the store."

Even with her back to him, she could feel his shock. He clearly hadn't expected her to treat the episode just as casually as he did. She was halfway across the garden before he found his voice. The cold air carried it so clearly she could hear the anger, the frustration, that filled it.

"Meggie?" It was a cross between an order and a question.

She kept walking, left foot in front of right....

"Megan!" Turning slowly, she looked blankly at him through the darkness.

"It's Krista, isn't it? That's what's bothering you." He sounded impatient. "Listen, Meggie, I know how it looks. But I can make it all right. I just need time. Will you just wait—"

She shuddered as she breathed in the wet, cold air. She knew what kind of waiting he meant. Waiting for a whispered phone call, a stolen meeting, a frenzied groping. Mouthed promises of better days ahead, all honey-eyed, soothing lies. Patrick Kelly had probably asked her mother to wait, too, and wait and wait . . . but the baby hadn't been willing to wait.

No! She couldn't stand it. "No. No, I won't. Let's just forget this ever happened, Ford. I'm the shopkeeper who's going to raise ten thousand dollars for the Chadbourne & Kelly coffers. That's all there is between us."

"I see." Even from this distance she could see his mouth grow thin, grim. "So we're right back where we started, on opposite sides of every issue. Tonight changed nothing?" He stood as still as an ice sculpture on the porch, one hand gripping the railing.

She shivered. What could have changed? She was still a nobody, and he was still the rich Mr. Chadbourne, who was getting ready to squire his debutante through the New Orleans social season. Did he think that she would accept whatever crumbs he could give her, after hours and on the sly?

"No," she answered, dully. "I can't see that it changed anything."

She half expected him to try to stop her. But he didn't. He just watched as she made her way numbly up the stairs to her rooms.

Sickeningly aware of that tall, still figure behind her, she almost had to pull herself up along the rail. Her legs grew heavier, and the door seemed to recede, like an elusive goal in a desperate nightmare. Somehow, though, she did reach it. She wrenched the door open just as her heart skidded. She felt as if she was losing her balance in a snow slip that grew and grew, until it became an avalanche and she was buried beneath it.

CHAPTER EIGHT

IRONICALLY, now that winter had settled into her heart, spring came sniffing at the edges of the city. It was perfect Mardi Gras weather. Not too sticky hot for energetic drinking and dancing. Not too cold for prancing through the parades in scanty costumes. The normal trickle of tourists swelled to a flood, making the sidewalks of the French Quarter almost unmaneuverable.

Megan tried to be glad. She hired Becky to tend the customers while she herself devoted every minute to plans for the open house. She tried to look at every customer as one more step toward victory. She tried not to care that it was never Ford.

She heard from Becky that he did sometime come to the store, but he obviously made it a point never to be there when Megan was. One day he left a new electronic cash register on the desk. Becky was ecstatic, declaring it made her job half the work and going on at some length about Ford's benevolence. Megan was more skeptical. Probably it just helped him keep track of the store's money, which was all he cared about anyway. Another day he left a new set of insurance policies in the drawer. All the coverage had been increased, for flood and fire and theft. Again Becky was impressed, Megan cynical. Far from being philanthropic, he was just protecting his interests. What could be more natural?

Though they both tried studiously, it was harder to avoid each other at home. Krista was staying at the big house, and several times during the next week or so, when Megan was pulling the old Subaru into the driveway, she met them, beautifully dressed and smiling, on their way out. A dinner at Antoine's, an evening at Preservation Hall, a party at one of the St. Charles Avenue mansions . . . Megan's throat closed up painfully. They were perfect together— Krista so pale and lovely, Ford tall and protective.

Each time, when they met in the backyard, they chatted lightly, and in her misery she couldn't remember anything they said. She knew only that Ford's demeanor was, if possible, even colder than her own. Krista tried to be friendly, but it was like trying to mold together two blocks of ice, and Ford shuttled her away quickly, leaving Megan to flee up her stairs as though demons were chasing her. And perhaps they were—demons of jealousy, of anger and . . .

Dizzy, she leaned over the kitchen counter and splashed cold water across her burning face. She might as well admit it—the demon of desire also ran hard at her heels. Her whole body ached for his touch, for him to fill her again with the pulsing light that brought such ecstasy and such release. It was just as she'd feared; he had unleashed a passion impossible to control.

But even knowing the battles she faced, she refused to wallow in guilt. She had not given herself lightly to Ford. However unwise it had proved to be, she had fallen in love with him. It was love, not lust, that had propelled her into his arms.

Never had she felt more empathy for her mother, from whom she obviously had inherited this capacity for passion. And never had she felt more anger toward selfish men like Ford Chadbourne and Patrick Kelly, men who thought they were entitled to take any woman they pleased, and did so as casually as they might pluck a sweet-smelling flower from the wayside.

Luckily the arduous effort required to pull the open house together kept her too busy to dwell on her predicament. By six o'clock on the Friday before Mardi Gras, which was also the eve of her open house, she was too tired to feel the dull ache of restless sensuality that had become so familiar.

It wasn't quite dark yet. The moon was no more than a light bleach spot on the steel-blue sky. But she was already planning to turn in early. It had been a long two weeks of sending out invitations, digging through merchandise, conferring with framers, arranging with caterers, but she was almost ready for the big night. All that was left was to pick up the last few things from the gallery and chill the champagne.

But that was tomorrow's work. Tonight was hers. Tonight she would rest. Her hair was spilling out of its high ponytail, and she wore smudges and streaks on her cheeks like war paint. Her light blue denim overalls were torn at the knees, and her yellow shirt was rolled up to reveal blackened elbows.

For the moment, though, her weary bones were just too tired to move, and she sat in the car, her head resting on one fist, and stared at the deepening blue of the evening sky. Her frozen dinners were melting on the seat beside her, but the flight of steps to the house looked too steep to climb.

If only she hadn't been so tired, she would have realized what a mistake it was to linger. The sound of the kitchen door roused her from her stupor, and she glanced, devastated, into her rearview mirror. Ford and Krista were emerging.

In the silver-blue glaze of twilight Krista's dress shimmered like moonbeams, though Megan realized it was probably just a delft-blue satin evening gown she had worn before. Ford, bending over Krista to clasp a glittering diamond chain around her slender neck, was all in white, like a fantasy hero. Their laughter rippled toward her like a purling stream.

Oh, no! She cast her eyes around frantically—what could she do? Enough silver light still hung in the sky for them to see her clearly. And Ford's Ferrari was parked right next to her car, so it would do no good simply to hunker down in her seat. Trapped, she decided that action was better than inaction and pushed open the car door.

"Hi," she called. Gathering her damp packages up in both arms, she headed briskly for the steps. "Going out? Well, it's a beautiful night for it. Have a good time!" That should do it—polite, but inviting no further discourse.

She almost made it. She was halfway up the narrow stairs when the TV dinners tore through the soggy bottom of the paper bag. Groceries tumbled like a rockslide. She froze, horrified.

She could almost hear Ford's sigh of exasperation. "I'll get them," she said hastily, scrambling down the steps, picking up cans of green beans as she went. But Ford had been bred as a gentleman, at least in all the superficial niceties, and in spite of his formal dress, he was stooping over, too, scooping up the oranges that had rolled to his feet. The two of them met halfway. His arms were laden with half-melted boxes of chicken Kiev and seafood linguini, but his eyes looked frozen solid.

"Open the door," he said. "I'll put these inside for you."

"That's okay," she insisted, reaching with her fingertips for his burden. "I'll do it."

He made a low sound of annoyance. "Open the door, dammit," he said harshly. "All I want to do is put these things in your refrigerator before they melt all over me."

"Oh, Megan, what a shame," Krista called up, her voice sounding genuinely distressed. "Ford, do help her. I'll wait in the car, okay?"

There was nothing to do but to unlock the door. In silence Ford entered ahead of her and began stacking the frozen dinners in the freezer.

"You might not want to eat these. They look pretty soft." His voice was businesslike. He dropped the oranges into the vegetable bin with a tinny bang. "These should be okay."

She wanted to thank him, but she didn't seem to have a voice. She stood just inside the door, arms still full of cans. It was the first time he had been inside her house since that night when they...since New Year's Eve. The edges of the cans cut into her breast, and she realized she had been squeezing them...

"Here, give me those." He pulled them from her stiff arms and slid them roughly into the cabinet.

"Ford..."

He turned around, his movements harsh. "What?"

She stared at him blankly. What had she been going to say? There was nothing to say. She couldn't say that her stomach was doing somersaults, that her knees were shaking, that her heart was aching. She couldn't say anything at all.

But he was still waiting. "What?" he repeated impatiently.

"Nothing. Just that I'm sorry."

Her answer seemed to disappoint him. He let his eyes roam up and down her disheveled body and then brought them up to her face. His brows pulled together sardonically in the center, and one side of his mouth went up in a mirthless smile.

"Yeah," he said. "Me, too."

And somehow, as he pushed past her toward the door, she knew neither of them had been talking about groceries.

BY THE TIME the hands of her clock had crawled to midnight, she was all cried out. She was clean, finally, and her hair was brushed into sleek control. She'd forced herself to eat an orange and had forced herself to get in bed. But she hadn't been able to force herself to go to sleep.

Like a self-pitying Cinderella she had sat cross-legged under the covers and wept because her fairy godmother hadn't come. Wept because she'd had to stand there in her rags and watch while another sparkling princess roared off into the night with her prince. Wept because, like a fool, like a self-destructive, masochistic fool, she had let herself fall in love where no love was returned. And it hurt. Oh, god, it hurt.

But by midnight the box of Kleenex tissues was empty and she was tiring of feeling sorry for herself. Crying was a waste of time, she lectured herself. A little self-respect, please . . .

Finally, by one o'clock, she was ready to face two things, two things no Cinderella ever really wanted to face. There were no fairy godmothers. And there were no princes.

She tossed her hair back defiantly and leaned against the cold brass headboard. Okay. She had faced them. So where did that leave her?

For one thing, it left her knowing she was going to have to be her own fairy godmother. If she wanted miracles in her life, she was going to have to work for them. Like tomorrow's open house. No magic wand could make that a success. It would take hard work. And it wouldn't help to sit up all night worrying and weeping, and end up too tired to show the buyers a confident face.

As for the prince—well, that would take some more time. The tears threatened again, as she wrapped her hands over the emptiness that gnawed at her midsection. A lot more time....

The rapping at her door was startling, falling as it did into the intense quiet of her darkened apartment. She twisted to get a better look at the clock. One-thirty? Who would be rapping at her door at one-thirty?

She couldn't tell whether it was fear or hope that clutched at her heart. A lot of strange people roamed the streets of New Orleans during Mardi Gras. She lay quietly, hoping the thundering of her heart couldn't be heard on the other side of the door.

The rapping sounded again, a quick, demanding rat-a-tat-tat that was slightly surreptitious even while it was insistent. Whoever it was didn't want to be heard, except by Megan. But they wanted in. Not just wanted—they *demanded*, with brusque knuckles, that she let them in.

Somehow, at that moment, when she identified that surreptitious quality, she knew. Her heart sliding in her chest, she slipped out of the bed, her short white cotton nightshirt hugging her thighs, and tiptoed toward the door. She had her hand on the knob when his low voice pierced the silence.

"Megan. Open the door. I want to talk to you."

Her hand froze. It was the voice she had expected to hear, but Ford's usual mellow tones were different tonight, and instinctively she knew why. He had been drinking. Somewhere out there, at some whirling, laughing, torch-lit ball, he had been drinking. His voice was not slurred, not sloppy—but, then, she wouldn't have expected liquor to make him sloppy. Instead it was just a little rougher than usual, a little more autocratic and arrogant.

He rapped again, his knuckles sounding louder on the wood, irritated at being thwarted. "I know you're in there, Megan. Open the door."

Resting her forehead against the smooth wood on the door, she shut her eyes. Every nerve inside her body said *open it*. Once it was unlatched, he would burst in and gather her up into his strong arms. She shivered, lost in the vivid imagining. She could almost smell the whiskey on his labored breath, could almost feel the warmth with which he would envelop her.

Her legs were alternately hot and cold, as though two conflicting tides swept through her, battering her, and her heart was pounding so hard she could feel it. *Open the door,* the dark currents and crashing waves insisted.

But her head said no. And again no. Wasn't this exactly how she had warned herself it would be? Even now Krista would be at the big house, hanging up her pretty blue gown and thinking fondly of her beautiful evening and her handsome escort. In her innocence she wouldn't believe that Ford was standing out here in the darkness, driven by desires she'd never glimpsed, knocking stealthily on Megan's door.

Trying to shut out the image, she squeezed her eyes so hard that colored dots swarmed behind her lids. It was all so tawdry. . . so painfully different from the cataclysmic joining of souls that she had so naively imagined their one night to be.

"Megan—Megan, listen to me." His voice had dropped to a low, coaxing note, and she stiffened, bracing herself to resist. "Let me in. I need you. And I know you need me. I could feel it tonight, when I came in . . ." His mouth must have been very near the door. She could hear each word as clearly as if it had been spoken against her ear. "We can work it out, Meggie. Let me in."

Oh, god, he had the silver tongue of an angel. Or of a devil. The muscles of her abdomen constricted in a rippling spasm, and in silent desperation she wrapped her hands across her chest, as though afraid that they might of their own volition reach out and twist the knob. Her heart pounded against her arms, and her knees grew hot and sparkly, as if her very bones were on fire. What power! The mere sound of his voice could make her weak with need.

Suddenly the door shook under her damp forehead as he slammed his fists against it in one muffled burst of frustration. She pulled back, startled by the swift change of mood.

"Damn it, Megan, what are you made of?" He cursed again. The desire that had driven him here was obviously driving him mad. His voice was thick and tormented. "Why are you doing this to me? To us?"

A silence stretched the air so thin it seemed about to break. When she didn't answer, he sighed heavily, raggedly.

"All right, then," he finally said in a low, stony voice. "But if I leave now, Megan, I'm not coming back. I won't crawl—do you hear me? I won't beg."

More silence. She breathed deeply through her mouth, hoping he couldn't hear her. She could almost imagine that she heard his labored breathing, even through the door.

"I said do you hear me?" The question was full of tightly reined rage.

When she didn't answer, he must have turned away. His heels scraped hard against the concrete and down the stairs. As she listened to his roughly retreating footsteps, she slithered down the door, her cotton nightshirt hunching up behind her as it snagged on the wood grain. Her knees could hold her no longer.

Then the footsteps died away in the night. He was gone. She had won. She had resisted him. She hugged her shins, dipping her trembling chin to her knees. Yes, she had *won*. A warm tear found its way down her cheek and onto her leg. So why did it feel so much like losing?

MEMORY LANE was closed Saturday morning, so that she and Becky could get ready for the open house, which was to begin in the late afternoon. Most of the other stores in the French Quarter were closed for the long weekend. It was easy to see why. Merrymakers whistled, hooted and laughed as they thronged against the narrow confines of the old streets, and most merchants just didn't think it was worth the risk—why let revelers intent on mindless hedonism shatter a priceless Ming?

Megan couldn't afford the luxury of shutting up shop for long, and she intended to be open again Sunday and Monday and even the great day itself, Fat Tuesday. She'd have to risk it. She needed the business.

So tomorrow the crowds would come, but this morning it was a luxury to work in relative quiet behind locked doors. Gathering up her supplies, she set to work. Several of the finished pictures still needed to be hung, and she measured the wall carefully for one, a nail ready between her teeth.

She tried to concentrate. But out of the corner of her eye she could still see the revelers outside. Everyone was laughing, but the laughter was muffled by her closed doors, and it was a little like watching a surreal silent movie. Cleopatra kissed Charlie Brown. Tweedle-Dum and Tweedle-Dee waltzed by with Henry the Eighth. A pirate cradled a sleeping clown in his arms.

Suddenly Megan put down her hammer and yardstick and walked toward the window. A tiny breeze of wistfulness passed over her. It was so alive out there. In the brilliant sunlight a thousand rhinestones burned orange and blue; gold and silver-threaded cloth winked and sparkled; and dazzling smiles transformed the most mundane faces into beauties.

She smiled at a buccaneer who had waved at her through the glass. She'd seen many Mardi Gras before, but never had the gaiety seemed so infectious, never had the beat of marching bands called so personally to her.

Her frown deepened. Being here felt good—and at the same time disturbing. What had happened to her famous control? It was as though the fire Ford had started with his lovemaking had burned away the protective layering in which she had wrapped herself.

Gratefully she heard the key turning in the lock. Good—she needed some company. Her thoughts were getting morbid.

The laughter increased momentarily as Becky opened the door.

"Wow!" Becky swiftly latched the door behind her. The roar subsided again. "What a mob! Sorry I'm late, but frankly I was lucky to get here in one piece."

"That's okay. We've still got about an hour before the guests arrive, and everything's just about ready anyhow." Shaking off her own thoughts with an effort, Megan finally noticed Becky's clothes. "You look fantastic," she said slowly. "But you'd better refresh my memory. Did we decide to wear costumes tonight?"

Becky fluffed up her dress, a gauzy concoction of pink and green that made her look like the Sugar Plum Fairy. "No, *we* didn't decide," she answered, a defiant gleam in her brown eyes. "*I* decided." She held up a small vanity case. "And I brought one for you, too."

Megan opened her mouth to protest, but Becky cut her off. "I don't want to hear any arguments. It's Mardi Gras, for pity's sake. We may have to work, but there's no law that says we can't have fun while we do it."

A slow smile lifted the corners of Megan's mouth. No, there wasn't any law against having fun. Oh, there might be one in Ford Chadbourne's three-piece world, just as he had a law against sentiment, but there wasn't one here in New Orleans, in her world.

"Well, let's see what you've got."

Becky whooped with victorious laughter and pulled out the dress. Megan's smile broadened. It was perfect. She had been fearing a typical Mardi Gras costume, whose primary characteristic was a blatant display of female skin. But this was beautiful, a turn-of-the-century commencement gown, black lace over oyster silk. Excited, she pressed it to her breast, holding out the huge puffed sleeves, which were caught in the middle of the upper arm with a black velvet ribbon, and swirling the full, floor-length skirt.

"Oh, I love it," she said, rubbing her hands across the soft lace. "It's perfect, Becky. Thanks!"

When she put it on, she felt magnificent. The dress belonged here, among all these unique old things, and it belonged on her. Made for a day when hourglass figures were the ideal, it accommodated her full breasts and tiny waist without any hint of vulgarity. The lace was as black as her hair, and the satin was as pale as her skin. And somehow the flushed red of her cheeks and lips looked right, too, as though they were put there, like softly fired rubies, for ornament.

Harry was the first to arrive, and his admiring stare brought an even deeper flush to her cheek. Harry was hardly the man of her dreams, but he was a good-looking male, and such a dramatic response was flattering from anyone.

"Hey, Megan, you look—you look—"

His awed stumblings were interrupted by the arrival of several other customers, including Mr. Hamilton, a tall man in black who owned several restaurants downtown. What a lucky break that he had been able to come!

"Thanks, Harry. That's sweet." Smiling, Megan patted his arm as she went to greet the newcomers, leaving Becky to give him champagne. Her spirits were rising, as surely as if a helium balloon had been tied to her heart. The evening was going to be success. She could feel it. Watch this, Mr. Chadbourne....

Deepening her smile, she moved toward the man in black, who had just lit a monstrous, foul-smelling cigar. She frowned quickly. Smoking wasn't ever allowed in Memory Lane... But she hated to risk offending him. Rumor had it he was planning to redecorate all of his restaurants, and several of her best arrangements had been concocted with him in mind.

She steeled herself to ignore the odor and met him with a smile and a small crystal bowl that would do as an ashtray in a pinch. But even that precaution wasn't enough. He was too careless to always notice when his cigar needed tipping. She tried not to wince as some gray ashes rained into the old carpet and kept sweetly extolling the many virtues of antiques as restaurant decor.

He seemed almost persuaded, although he didn't commit himself. Others did, though. Over the next few hours dark settled on the Quarter, but inside the store was bright with good spirits.

Megan flitted from one laughing group to another, feeling more like a hostess than a saleswoman as she gave advice and shared the histories of the featured merchandise. Yes, she told one customer, that was an authentic nineteen-hundreds map of New Orleans, framed inside a border of postcards of turn-of-the-century houses. The man, an architect, nodded, smiled and bought it. Yes, she told another, those were old movie photographs featuring famous costumes, framed on a backdrop of ivory Battenberg lace. The boutique owner bought it.

She was helping Evan Tandy, who owned a tavern in the French Quarter, decide whether he wanted a collage of antique playing cards or an Early American print when Ford arrived.

All at once the merry chatter that had filled the room seemed to fade out. Her heart pumped furiously, sending too much blood coursing through her cheeks, and the lace seemed to crawl disagreeably across the back of her neck.

Krista hung prettily on Ford's arm, and Megan saw instantly that they had stopped by on their way to something else, something formal. Krista's yellow satin dress was simple but elegant—how many suitcases full of these treasures had she brought with her?—and her long mint-green satin cloak had a high, winged collar that buttoned with a huge creamy pearl at her throat.

As her heartbeat slowed down to a normal pace and her hearing returned, Megan came to enough to notice Becky at her elbow, champagne glasses in hand. She handed one to Megan.

"La Blonde?" Becky's brown eyes were wide, staring dramatically toward the door as she sipped the bubbling liquid.

Megan nodded. "Krista Kelly. Of Chadbourne & Kelly."

Shaking her own blond head mournfully, Becky sighed. "Oh dear. This is serious. I think I hear my heart breaking."

Megan nudged her with one elbow. "Oh, I don't think so. If you hear anything, it's just your ego tumbling a notch or two. I *told* you there were other blondes in the world...."

"But you didn't tell me she was really prettier than I am," Becky complained, watching the pair carefully. "How depressing! And look—even Hands-on Harry has noticed."

Megan looked. Harry was already at Krista's side. And Ford—Ford was looking at *her*. His green eyes were dark, the brows pulled straight across them. His lips were set straight, too, not showing any expression at all. There was no anger in his look, no condemnation, no violent emotion of any kind—last night's midnight visit might never have happened at all. And yet she couldn't forget. A shiver raced down the middle of her back, from her neck to her tailbone, as she met his gaze.

With only a light touch to her elbow Ford pulled Krista away from Harry easily and led her straight to where

Megan stood, as paralyzed as the sparrow at the approach of the hawk.

"Megan, everything looks beautiful," Krista enthused innocently, giving her a warm hug. "What a wonderful idea! I see so many things already that I'd just love to have."

Megan tried to return the warm embrace, to match the bright smile, but she was too conscious of Ford's unsmiling presence.

"Please," she said as warmly as her frozen lips could manage, "let me know what you'd like. I'd love to make it a gift."

"Oh, no!" Krista looked horrified. "You can't do that! This rat here has told me what he's doing, about the deadline he gave you." She shot Ford a hesitant but disapproving look, which, to Megan's astonishment, he accepted with a hint of a grin. "So...you must let me buy. We have to teach this stubborn man a lesson."

Ford tucked his grin away, but a deep dimple revealed that he was still amused. Irrationally, envy pricked at Megan's heart. The understanding between Krista and Ford was so deep that he would accept anything from her.

"Teach away, ladies," he said solemnly. "I am your most eager pupil."

Krista laughed shyly. "What a fib! He hates to lose, Megan, and he's a very *bad* loser. He doesn't get enough practice at it." She took Megan's arm and moved toward the side wall, where most of the pictures had been hung. "Now. Come tell me how much your postcard calendar over there costs. And that pretty one with the christening dress in it. I just love it."

Several hundred dollars later, they returned to where Ford and Becky were sipping champagne.

"Well, what did *you* buy, Ford?" Krista pointed her finger into the pleated white shirt that gleamed under Ford's tuxedo.

Horrified, Megan cut in. "Krista, surely you don't think that Ford would buy anything here? It would be ridicul—"

"I bought the diary," he put in smoothly.

"The diary?" Confused, Megan looked toward Becky, whose pink lips were pursed in a smug smirk.

"Yes," Becky said, her voice as smug as her lips. "He bought the Civil War diary."

Megan shook her head in distress. She didn't want to sell the diary to *anyone*, but especially not to Ford Chadbourne. "But that's not for sale yet, Becky. I have to look it up in Sotheby's lists, to see what to charge for it." She turned to Ford. "It's on consignment from a friend. He is going to let me set the price, so I have to be fair."

He laughed and put his arm around Krista companionably. "What did I tell you? She doesn't have a single cutthroat instinct. See why she'll never make it to the Fortune Five Hundred?"

Megan's cheeks flamed. How dare he ridicule her here, in front of them all? He didn't *deserve* to have the diary. It was too beautiful, too full of all the emotions he'd never understand. He'd never understand the pathos of the infant daughter deprived of a father. Not like she did. He'd probably just stash it in his safe-deposit box until it appreciated enough for him to make a tidy profit on it. Whereas *she* would cherish it, if she could afford it.

"I'm sorry," she said stiffly. "But that diary is not for sale. You knew that, Becky."

Becky scowled. "No, you just said you didn't know what you were going to ask for it. So I told him that, and he said he would put five hundred dollars down on it and pay you the rest when you'd finished researching it. I have his check here." She dug out the paper from her pocket and waved it under Megan's nose. "Five hundred dollars—kind of like lay-away."

Megan's anger hardened. And the rest later, when it would be too late to help her win the bet. He probably thought that was amusing. God, he was the most calculating...

"I'm sorry," she repeated through clenched teeth. "The diary is not for sale." She turned to him, the muscles in her face stiff and hard. "You must not have looked at it very carefully, Ford. It's not your kind of thing. It's a collection of letters from a soldier to the child he has never seen. It's all about memories and loneliness, about forgiveness and love...."

"I see." A pulse beat in his temple, and she knew he was angry. Even Krista was frowning nervously. "But then it doesn't sound like *your* kind of thing either, does it?" He peeled the check from Becky's fingers and pocketed it.

He took Krista's arm. "Well, never mind. On second thought it probably *will* cost me too much. So I'll just wait until next week. Then I can have it for free."

CHAPTER NINE

By the time Megan struggled out of bed and in to work on Sunday, Becky had already opened up. She would have liked to chat, but the store was full of customers, so she settled herself down to work on the books.

After several hours she sighed, frowning at the figures, which seemed to wriggle in front of her tired eyes. Last night had been a success, but had it been enough? She had spent so much on the open house....

And today hadn't helped much. No wonder the other merchants didn't bother staying open on Mardi Gras weekend, she thought in frustration as she eyed the browsers who clogged the store. She would bet her right arm that not one of them intended to buy.

Well, Tuesday it would be over, one way or the other. Judging from these figures, it would be close. Right now she was about a thousand dollars short. And that was gross sales—she'd already factored in the overhead.

Close, but— She bit her lip. Normal business wouldn't bring in that much, not if most of the customers were browsers. Her only hope was that one of the seeds she'd planted last night would take root quickly. Maybe Mr. Hamilton, the cigar-smoking restaurateur? He had seemed interested.

Maybe she should call him. She glared at the telephone, hating all the maneuvering. She didn't want to sweet-talk the man in black. She wanted to go home and go to bed.

But in Ford's inimitable words, being tired was a luxury she couldn't afford. Her hand was on the telephone, ready to dial Mr. Hamilton's number, when it rang.

Becky raced over to get it, clearly welcoming any escape from the boredom of following the browsers around.

"Memory Lane," she chirped. Seconds later her face fell comically, and pressing her palm to the mouthpiece, she handed it to Megan. "It's for you," she said dolefully. "Mr. Wrong."

Ford? Megan took the telephone with some trepidation. He was sure to be angry about last night, and though she knew she had been out of line, she wasn't feeling conciliatory.

"Yes?" She spoke coolly.

"I'll tell you what." He didn't bother to identify himself. "I'll count to three slowly, and then we'll both say 'I'm sorry' at the same time. Okay? One . . . two . . ."

"I'm sorry," she jumped in. "There's no need to be patronizing. I realize I spoke out of turn last night. We both know that the diary, like everything else in this store, is yours already." She leaned her forehead against her hand, winding her fingers into her curls. "It's just that I get defensive for these things. I care about them. I want to see them go where they'll be appreciated, not to someone who—"

"Hold on," he warned. "Don't overheat. You might say something you'll have to apologize for tomorrow."

She pressed her lips together. He was right. She had been about to be rude again. Why couldn't she control her tongue? She swallowed the rest of her words and took a deep breath.

"That's better." He obviously interpreted her silence correctly. "Now, with that behind us, let's move forward." He took on a crisp tone again. "Our deadline for the bet is Tuesday night, you know. Krista thinks a celebration is in order."

She almost choked on her indignation. What gall he had! "Aren't you a bit premature? You haven't seen the figures yet. When you do, you may not feel like celebrating."

"Oh, yes I will." He sounded definite. "I don't have any idea where we stand financially, and I don't really give a damn right now. I think we should celebrate just surviving the godforsaken bet at all. Whoever wins. It was Krista's idea, you know."

Oh, it was? She clenched the receiver, jamming it against her ear. "I think not."

"Come on, Megan." He sounded annoyed. "Do it for Krista? She wants you to come. She likes you. And she was quite decent last night, I thought. Don't you owe her this small favor?"

She hesitated. Again, maddeningly, he was right. Krista had gone out of her way to help. It would be ungrateful to decline.

And she wasn't even sure she wanted to decline. Krista probably would be returning to New York soon, and Megan might never see her again. In spite of the whole horrible mess, in spite of the fact that she probably would never burden Krista with the truth about their relationship, even in spite of the envy that sometimes crept in and soured her feelings, Megan knew she'd never regret having met her half sister. Being connected to another human being by a blood tie—even an unacknowledged one—somehow made the world less lonely.

And Krista was a special person, gentle and unaffected for all her wealth. No wonder Ford cherished her so.

"All right," she agreed reluctantly, her heart torn. She wanted to see Krista. And, heaven help her, she even wanted to see Ford. But could she bear to see them *together*? "I'll join you. What time?"

SHE SHOULD have known. She really should have known.

The minute she opened her door and saw Ford standing there alone, she wanted to kick herself for being so gullible.

Krista wasn't coming. Probably Ford had never even invited her. But why should that be a surprise? If she'd given it a moment's logical thought, she'd have realized that Ford would never waste such a romantic night on a platonic threesome.

For a minute Megan didn't know whether to laugh or cry. It was so predictable. But as the cold air blew against her hot cheeks, she could tell she was flushing with indignation. He must have realized it, too—his full lips were pressed together in a knowing smile.

The look enraged her, obliterating any impulse to cry. He thought it was funny, did he? He probably imagined her trembling with trepidation, not trusting herself to be alone with him for fear her desire would overpower her senses.

Well, baloney! She'd show him that he was not only *under*estimating her—he was also *over*estimating himself. Raising her brows, she drew herself up, arranging the folds of her full black velvet skirt and clipping on her gold hoop earrings.

"Couldn't Krista make it?" she asked equably. "What a shame."

"Isn't it?" Ford's voice rippled with counterfeit, and her annoyance hardened. "It seems she received a call-out invitation from the Comus Krewe. She just couldn't pass up the chance."

Megan almost believed him. Any invitation to one of the Mardi Gras balls was worth treble its weight in gold. A call-out invitation, which meant a Krewe member wanted to dance with you, was an incomparable social coup.

"A call-out? How lovely for her," she observed pleasantly, pushing back the sleeve of her black velvet turtleneck to check her watch. "Well, if we want to see the parade, we'd better go."

One side of his mouth quirked up. "I suppose we had."

As they maneuvered the steps, she willed iron into the arm he took in his. She would *not* let it shake. He must see how strong her resolve had become. If necessary she would turn to granite rather than tremble under his touch. She remembered the Greek myth she had learned in school, of the goddess who turned into a laurel tree to avoid seduction.

Finally her sense of humor took over. She chuckled at the thought of her black curls transforming themselves into laurel leaves. What a mess! A little willpower would be much simpler.

"Did I miss something?" After helping her into the low-slung leather seats of the Ferrari, he slid in and turned toward her, his brows arched quizzically. "Something strike you funny?"

She smiled back. "Oh, not really. I guess maybe I'm just finally getting into the Mardi Gras spirit."

"Good." He started the engine. "It's about time. Let's leave business behind for tonight and have some fun."

Business. The very word brought back the nibble of anxiety. When she had talked to Becky at about four o'clock this afternoon, they were a few hundred dollars short of their target. But there was still hope, Becky had said—Mr. Hamilton, the restaurateur Megan had called last night, had just arrived.

Unfortunately that was no guarantee. Mr. Hamilton had explained that even if he chose to buy, he would need custom-made arrangements. Megan had left instructions with Becky to ask for a deposit that was at least one penny larger than the amount they needed to meet Ford's goal. Please, Mr. Hamilton, she prayed silently, put down your cigar long enough to place an order.

She sighed, trying to keep her optimism in check. It looked good—but she'd be happier when she could get to a telephone and check with Becky. She didn't want anything to go wrong.

"Don't you even want to know how we're doing?" she asked Ford.

"No, I really don't." He didn't look at all worried, though he must have suspected what her good spirits implied. "In fact, I don't want to hear another word about it tonight." He gave her a clear, green glance before turning back to the street. "It's Mardi Gras. Let's make it a night to remember."

Goose bumps broke out on her arms, even under the protective layer of velvet. The evening wasn't that cold, so it must have been the peculiar, intense tone of his deep voice.... Perhaps she had been wrong to laugh at that myth. The spike of desire that drove into her now was no laughing matter.

Sobered, she turned her face to the window, watching the houses float by her vision in the moonlight. Hard to believe, really, that the great day was already here. Fat

Tuesday, the last day before Lent, when fasting and denial would replace merriment and self-indulgence. The religious significance of the holiday had paled through the years, lost in all the glitter, but it took on a new meaning for her now.

Suddenly she thought she understood what Ford meant when he said that this should be a night to remember. It was a gentle reminder that this was the end, not just of Mardi Gras, not just of their bet, but also of their time together. Tomorrow, whatever happened with Memory Lane, Ford would wing his way back to his boardroom. And then he, like Mardi Gras, would be a memory.

She shot him a searching glance, but all she could see was his rugged profile, his square jaw, his firm lips. It revealed nothing that might have let her delude herself that he felt any pain at the prospect of leaving. . . .

No, she was a fool to consider it possible. But the knowledge of his indifference didn't stop her from remembering with earthshaking clarity how those lips had felt against her skin, how his hot breath had mingled with hers.

She squeezed her hands in her lap, locked into the memory. Would she never know that feeling again? Would she never again lie in the arms of the man she loved? *Love*—it was still true. This burning, dizzying feeling wasn't just passion—it was love.

And it was forever. The end of the bet wouldn't change it. Even his leaving her wouldn't change it. She turned away. That left only tonight. Only this one last torch-lit night.

They were nearing the parade route now, and he sidled the Ferrari into a parking space.

"Let's walk from here," he said. "We won't do any better."

They were just in time. Somehow, by deftly angling through the layers of spectators, Ford managed to find a spot close enough to see the street.

As the parade approached, she caught her breath. Surely it had never seemed so utterly splendid before. But tonight, with her emotions achingly near the surface, she had to fight back tears as the solemn flambeaux carriers appeared.

"Oh, Ford," she cried softly, though he probably couldn't hear her over the roar of the crowd. It was, she thought, holding her hand at her throat, the most beautiful sight she had ever seen. The leaping, flaring, golden torches, carried high above their heads...within minutes, the street was transformed, the darkness banished by the glowing arc of dancing light.

"Throw me something, Mister!"

From his perch high atop his father's shoulders, a little boy's excited cry filled the crisp night air. Miraculously the marchers seemed to see his eager hands even in that sea of reaching hands. Golden doubloons fell like rain around them. Her eyes still misty, Megan watched as the falling coins landed at her feet.

"Here, honey." Bending quickly, she scooped up several of the golden discs and pressed them into the boy's tiny hand before the other eager revelers could reach them.

The father thanked her, but the boy's smile, which was as bright as the coins themselves, was her real reward. She beamed back. She could well imagine how magical this all seemed to a child. She felt a bit like a child herself.

"But now, for the pretty lady..." Ford's hard hands were on her shoulders, and she turned toward him, her face shining.

Again she caught her breath. His face was golden, too, in the glow of the torches, and his eyes were fiery. Reaching with long arms over her head, he draped strings of beads around her neck, slowly, one strand at a time. There must have been a dozen, in all colors of the rainbow.

"For me?" She felt as exultant as the little boy had looked. How had he managed to catch so many? They were just cheap plastic—at any other time, in any other place, they would have been junk. But tonight they were as precious as ropes of rubies and emeralds. Every woman who stood wreathed in them felt like a princess, she thought.

And she was no exception. With shaking hands she fingered the cool plastic that lay in vivid stripes of color against her black velvet blouse.

"Oh, I love them. I've never caught anything before. How do they look?"

Unsmiling, he touched the beads, too, running the tips of his fingers across the strands. "Radiant," he said softly. "You look radiant."

Though they had begun at opposite sides of her neck and followed separate paths across the twisted strands, their fingers met at the bottom of the loop, where the beads curved low on her breast. Without a word, as though compelled by an ungovernable force, their hands closed, the warm, yielding flesh of their fingers tangling around the hard pebbles of the necklaces.

Her heart was thundering against her hand, and she knew he could feel it, too. His grip grew tighter, until her blood throbbed in her fingertips and the beads dug into her palm.

His gaze never dropped from hers. The din of the parade faded out, though the torches seemed to leap into a fiercer light, surrounding him with a lambent glow. She held her breath, as though by doing so she could stop the moment from slipping away.

But of course, she couldn't. A laughing young woman careened into them in her eagerness to catch a "throw." Megan stumbled, and their hands parted as Ford reached out to steady her. She began to breathe again, the roaring crowd again filled her ears, and the moment was gone.

"Sorry!" The young woman reemerged, her hands dripping with plastic beads, and she grinned conspiratorially. "I just *had* to get some. You got lucky, too, huh?"

Nodding, Megan smiled back. She shouldn't be angry—she should be grateful to be reminded that she wasn't the only plastic princess out tonight. It wouldn't be smart to let the music and the lights intoxicate her. At the stroke of midnight, all this would disappear.

"There's Comus." Ford pointed toward the street, where a sparkling float was rumbling by.

A new roar rose out of the crowd as Comus, their appointed God of Revelry, came into view. The masked god, who rode high above them, lifted his golden goblet, nodding his headdress of white plumes as he saluted to the right and the left.

"He's on his way to the ball," Ford said, leaning toward her to be heard over the noise. "Do you want to go?"

Megan wasn't sure she'd heard him correctly. To Comus's ball? *No one* could get tickets to Comus's ball . . .

"What?" she asked, frowning. She must have misunderstood.

He fished in his pocket and held out two tickets. "The ball. Do you want to go?"

She didn't know what to say. He probably expected her to be breathless with delight. It was the chance of a lifetime. Only the most socially correct would be allowed to attend Comus's ball.

She bit her lip. The only hitch was that she didn't particularly want to go. She stared at the tickets—how could she explain to him that this had never been one of her dreams? In fact, until she had met him, she had never given "high society" any thought at all. She was happy with her own life, her own friends.

But he would never understand, never believe that she'd rather just be with him, alone somewhere, sharing a dozen oysters and listening to a little Dixieland jazz.

"Well?" His tone was teasing, and he kept his arm around her. "Do you want to go or not?"

"No, not really," she said reluctantly. But as soon as she spoke the words she realized how selfish they were. She shouldn't let her own indifference keep *him* from going. It might not be her world, but it was his. "But I'll go, if it's important to you...."

To her surprise, he grinned and tossed the tickets into the air. They were snatched up before they hit the ground.

"Thank goodness," he said. "I can't tell you how I was hoping you'd say that."

Catching her hand, he abruptly pulled her away from the parade. "I've got a much better idea," he called over his shoulder. Suddenly he seemed in a great hurry, and she followed as best she could, her full velvet skirt billowing out behind her as they threaded through the crowds.

The night had turned cold, and the breeze was sharp against her cheeks as she rushed after him. They quickly left Canal Street behind and finally slowed to a walk as they veered onto Bourbon Street. She clutched his hand, surprised at the sight before them. A different magic reigned here, where the untamed sounds of trumpets and saxophones spilled out of every door, creating a reckless cacophony of sensuality. Neon signs beckoned, and disappointment pricked at her. This wasn't what she wanted, this erotic mingling of liquor and laughter. Was this where he thought she belonged?

Finally, just as her breath was coming normally again, he tugged her down a softly shadowed corner, onto one of the narrow side streets. Here the raucous sounds of Bourbon Street were muted—and her heart lightened. He led her into a quiet, dimly lit courtyard restaurant she had never seen before.

It was perfect. Only a half dozen customers sat at the iron tables that formed a circle around a three-tiered fountain. Apparently the hushed elegance of this little hideaway didn't suit the Mardi Gras tourists, but Megan was enchanted.

She mutely smiled her approval and dropped onto one of the ancient wrought-iron chairs, drinking in the beauty that surrounded them. The vines that covered the crumbling brick walls were silvered with moonlight, and the unlighted fountain that murmured behind them seemed to cascade not plain water but some mysterious, liquid essence of the night.

Ford ordered for both of them. Megan didn't hear what he asked for, and though she ate, she didn't taste it when it came. Her senses registered that it was warm and succulent, that spicy steam rose into her nostrils; her mind knew only Ford.

Later she would remember that they had talked of little things, offering bits of information about themselves, small stories that were sad or funny. Their laughter was low and unhurried, but their hands met across the table, and their fingers stroked and twisted, as if restless to know more of each other.

When the food was taken away, she leaned forward, her chin on her hand. "What a wonderful place," she murmured. A series of saxophone notes disconnected themselves from Bourbon Street and floated toward them, like smoke rings on the air. "It's like being hidden away in a secret world."

He smiled, and his thumb stroked the palm of her hand. "Hadn't you ever been here before?"

She shook her head, looking around her dreamily. "No. I don't know how I missed it. I've lived in New Orleans all my life, and yet I never found this wonderful place."

"All your life?" He leaned forward, his face masked in the silver shadows. "But you lived with Natalie for only five years. I definitely got the impression this was *not* your home. What about your family? Do they live here, too?"

Instinctively she tried to ease her hand away, to draw back into herself and her carefully kept secrets. But his fingers tightened slightly.

"My mother's dead," she said carefully, braced by the warmth of those fingers. "She died when I was very little. I was brought up as a boarder at the convent school here in New Orleans."

His hand tightened further. "What about your father?"

She looked down at their hands, so tightly braided together, dark finger over light, strong finger alternating with small. They seemed inseparable. Surely on this magic night it would be possible to tell him the truth without splitting them apart.

"He's dead, too."

His eyes were liquid in the moonlight, and he dipped his head to drop a kiss on her knuckles. "I'm sorry," he said simply. "That must have been rough. Would you rather not talk about it?"

She shook her head. "No," she said. "I think perhaps it's time we did talk about it. Past time, really. I should have told you from the first. I should have told Natalie, too. I didn't even know my father had died until years after it happened. I didn't ever know my father. *You* knew him better than I did."

He drew back, his brows contracting over his eyes. "What?" His grip tightened so hard she winced. "What are you saying?"

The horror in his voice filled her with dismay. She had allowed herself to hope that it wouldn't matter to him, that there was a bond between them that would make their disparate backgrounds unimportant. But once again she might be wrong. Desperately, insanely wrong.

Her voice tightened as the misery sank deeper. "I'm talking about my father. Patrick Kelly."

His fingers suddenly relaxed their hold, as though the blood had drained out of them. She seized the opportunity to free her hand and dropped it into her lap, where she laced it into the other.

Ford's eyes were narrow. "Good god—are you asking me to believe that you are Patrick Kelly's child? But that would mean—" he waved the idea way with a rough hand. "That's nonsense. I knew him—I'd known him ever since I was a little boy. He was my father's partner. It just isn't possible."

"I'm not *asking* you to believe anything." She was trembling with anger, but she tried to keep her voice low. "I don't care what you believe. I can't imagine what possessed me to tell you in the first place. I should have known better."

He reached out to touch her shoulder, but she wrenched away, and he held his palm out in a gesture of pacification.

"Hey, settle down. I'm just saying that I knew Patrick Kelly, and the man I knew wasn't capable of such a thing."

She glared at him, her eyes gleaming daggers in the moonlight. "Not capable? Of fathering a child? Or is it that you think he wasn't capable of conducting a sleazy affair with some nobody from New Orleans? You of all people should know better than that!"

He shook his head impatiently. "Stop putting words in my mouth, Megan. I mean he wasn't capable of having a child that he didn't acknowledge. He was the most tender, caring father I'd ever seen. I knew him, I tell you. If he had fathered another child, he would have done something about it."

Her stomach was churning, the lovely dinner now making her feel slightly sick. "Oh, he did something about it. He paid my room and board at the convent. Apparently he thought it was enough. But you can say this for him—he always paid on time."

"Megan, stop it." Ford broke into her diatribe, his voice hard. "I don't know why your mother told you Patrick Kelly was your father, but—"

"She didn't. A private detective did. It didn't take him long—he just traced the tuition checks. How he got hold of them, I'll never know. But they came from Patrick Kelly, all right. Patrick James Kelly, of Chadbourne & Kelly, New York."

He ran his hands through his mahogany hair, obviously frustrated to the breaking point. "I don't understand," he muttered, almost to himself. "It's just not possible. Patrick would never...unless he didn't really believe you were his—"

Her anger exploded like one of the Mardi Gras fireworks, and she raked her chair back, scraping it against the bricks.

"Oh, of course," she cried bitterly. "It has to be my mother who was lying, doesn't it? It couldn't be the honorable Mr. Kelly. No one could possibly be a liar and a rich man at the same time—that's the way it works in your world, isn't it?"

She stood behind her chair, gripping the old black iron so hard she felt the paint flaking under her fingers.

"I've always known what kind of people you were— you Chadbournes and Kellys. Why do you think I never got in touch with any of you? I'm no prouder to have had such a man for a father than apparently he was to have me for a child! You all make me sick." The blood pounded toward her head, making the veins in her neck burn thick and hot. "You run around doing whatever you please, not caring whose life you wreck while you're at it. And then, when things get too tough, then you run back to your boardrooms and your wives and your debutantes...."

Her voice was ragged, and she pulled in a torn breath. "Well, go on, then, get out! I don't want you here, playing your selfish games with me. And don't flatter yourself that you'll be missed. I did fine without Patrick Kelly, and I'll do fine without you!"

Shaking off the hand he threw out to stop her, she turned sharply and ran down the street, blindly racing toward the music and the lights. She didn't know if he followed. She didn't care. She just wanted to get away.

Without thinking, she ran toward Memory Lane, as though it were the beacon and she the foundering ship. In her desperate flight she didn't realize how late it was, didn't realize that Mardi Gras had ground to a cold, lonely halt, until she heard the chimes of the St. Louis Cathedral. The round tones rose high above the smell of sour whiskey that hung like a stale miasma over the French Quarter. Midnight. The time of love and plenty had run out; the time of regret and atonement had begun. As the tones died out, she turned the final corner.

At first she thought her tear-blinded eyes deceived her. The frightening red halo around the window, the puffs of smoke—

Her legs stopped cold beneath her, though her heart still pounded in her ears. Memory Lane was on fire.

CHAPTER TEN

She hesitated only a fraction of a second, just long enough for the acrid smell of smoke to invade her nostrils. And then she plunged forward.

"Oh, no. Oh, god, no!" She wasn't sure whether she moaned the words or screamed them. All she heard were the sounds of fire—a low, hideous crackling, a dull rumble, an ominous hiss.

It must have started only minutes ago. Her ears strained for the sound of arriving sirens, but she heard nothing but the fire itself and the low tones of passersby who had stopped to see what all the commotion was about.

"Please," she called, her voice thin with desperation. "Please, call the fire department. Hurry."

Someone trotted off obediently, but the others stayed to stare as Megan raced back to the door. Through the window she could see a shifting orange stain behind the clouds of smoke, but she couldn't tell exactly what was burning, or where. Maybe it hadn't taken hold yet...

"Please. Let me be in time..." She groped for the doorknob and twisted, squinting her eyes and bracing herself for the explosion of heat.

But the door wouldn't budge. Opening her eyes, she saw a long arm, a broad shoulder, jamming the way.

Frantic, she pulled again, but she wasn't strong enough. "Oh, please, please, let me through," she moaned.

"Are you crazy, Megan? Don't touch that door."

It was Ford, his face dark with anger, his eyes reflecting the growing red stain just inside the window. The fire was getting bigger. How dare he try to stop her?

"Move away," she ground out between clenched teeth. "I have to get in. There's a fire. I have to, please...please, Ford, move and let me through."

His face growing darker, he pried her hand from the knob.

"Get hold of yourself, Megan. Let the fire department take care of it. They'll be here soon."

"It'll be too late," she bit back. "And they'll flood water all over the place, which will be just as disastrous for the stock as the fire itself. I have to put it out, Ford. It's the only way. Otherwise..." Her voice fell. "We'll lose everything."

"No, we won't," he said, his voice soothing but his hand frozen, unyielding, against the door. "It's insured, remember? I even increased the insurance. You won't lose a penny."

Megan stared at him, unable to believe her ears.

"Money? Do you think this is about *money*?" She wanted to slap him, but she concentrated her energy on trying to move his arm. "I don't give a damn about the money," she panted, furiously trying to wriggle past his rock-hard body. "It's not *money* that's burning up in there. It's not just more of your widgets. It's *people*, it's history...oh, Ford, the diary is in there!"

Clawing at his restraining hand, she turned a beseeching face up into his. But if she had hoped to move him, she had been a fool. His face was just as stony as ever.

"You could get killed, Megan. Would you let yourself get killed just to save those pieces of paper in there?"

She coughed, choking on tears and smoke. "Oh, god, why should I waste time trying to make you understand?" Tears ran in black rivulets down her cheeks. "You don't have any idea what I'm talking about, do you? I wish there *were* some money in there. Then you wouldn't be standing out here trying to stop me. You'd be in there, yourself. For money." Her voice grew shrill, and she coughed again. "Money! *That's* the only thing you understand, isn't it?"

A pulse beat violently in his temple, and she thought for a moment that he might hit her. She couldn't bring herself to care. She cared only about the smoke that grew ever thicker about the door, which was growing warm under her touch, as though the fire were creeping closer with every passing second. And it would be consuming everything in its path. The past was so fragile....

A new voice had been added to the murmur of onlookers. "Megan? I just got a call . . . said our block was on fire—"

"*Evans!* Thank god you're here." With no effort at gentleness Ford grabbed Megan by the shoulders and shoved her toward the street. Caught off guard she stumbled and fell into waiting arms. Harry?

"Hold on to her, Evans. She's being a damned fool— she's trying to go in." At the harsh words from Ford Harry's arms tightened automatically across Megan's collarbone, and she knew she was trapped. "Whatever you do, don't let go of her."

How she hated him at that moment! She writhed in Harry's arms. "Let go of me!"

"Megan, I can't." Harry sounded bewildered. "You weren't really trying to get in that hell hole, were you? The fire department is on its way—" His voice broke off with a gasp of horror. "Chadbourne—what the hell—"

Megan whipped around in time to see Ford's dark body disappearing into the red-rimmed doorway, his coat held over his head. She thought her knees would shatter beneath her, so great was the panic that shot through her body.

"Ford, no!" Now that the door had been swung open, she could see how impossible the situation was. It was like looking into the mouth of a monster—voracious red and orange tongues seemed to devour the very air that dared to enter. Heat billowed out to scorch her face.

"Oh, Ford," she whispered. "Ford, no."

Was this how he'd felt when *she* had wanted to open the door and fling herself into that boiling cauldron? Had he felt his heart bursting with fear and horror? Had an explosion of misery swept through him at the thought that he might lose his future to save sentimental scraps of the past? She heard a whimpering—it must have been her own. And then, just as the blackness cloaked her, she heard the swelling, building, scream of a siren....

SHE COULD hardly believe the birds were singing.

But why shouldn't they? It was a beautiful, flower-filled day, and nothing else mattered to the songbirds, not the charred heap of brittle ashes left inside the black walls of Memory Lane, and not the man who now lay broken on Natalie's four-poster bed.

As she stood at her window looking down on the deserted garden, Megan knew she should feel lucky. Though most of the things inside Memory Lane had burned to ashes, the firemen had been able to contain the fire to her store and had even been able to put it out before it destroyed the centuries-old building.

And most importantly, they had arrived in time to pull Ford from the flames, even after the window had burst, heaving the refectory table onto its side and pinning Ford beneath it. Harry had told her later, when she'd been brought home, washed and put to bed herself, that Ford had momentarily regained consciousness when they brought him out on the stretcher. His face was black with soot, contorted with pain. His only sentence had been, "Tell her I couldn't find it."

She knew what he had meant. The diary. A painful spasm twisted at her insides. What a fool she had been! No wonder he had been so angry. He'd understood long ago what she hadn't known until the moment his body had disappeared into the flames—that the past must not be allowed to ruin the present. He had tried to make her see it, too. But she had been too blind.

She fingered the black bow at the neck of her cardigan and swallowed hard over the painful knot in her throat. Yes, she had been too blind, and now, now that it was too late, she had to go and tell him how sorry she was for having been such a self-righteous, opinionated fool.

No wonder he'd preferred Krista to her. Megan forced herself to face the truth, and the truth was not flattering. His preference had probably had very little to do with their relative social standings. Krista was sunny and trusting, where Megan was judgmental and wary. Krista was forgiving, where Megan nursed her resentments relentlessly. Krista looked to the future, where Megan cursed the past.

She put her hands in front of her face, ashamed. What a mess she had made of things! When Becky had called early this morning, to report that Megan had won the bet before the fire broke out, the victory had seemed like ashes, too. Mr. Hamilton had put a huge down payment on a custom order, so technically, Megan had won. And yet, in reality, she knew she had lost everything.

Well, now it was time for her to start acting like a lady and go to thank him for trying to save her diary. Already it was almost noon, and she hadn't stopped by to see how he was faring.

She fluffed her blue and green ribbon-striped skirt, smoothed her cardigan down over it, took a deep breath and headed down the steps and across the garden.

At the kitchen door she hesitated again. Suppose she wasn't welcome here any more? Ford certainly had reason enough to hate her now, if he hadn't before. But she had to try. Even if he turned her away, decency demanded she make the effort.

She rapped lightly on the wood with one knuckle. If he was still sleeping, she didn't want to wake him. Just because she'd lain awake all night tortured by regrets didn't mean that he—

"Oh, Megan, I'm so glad you came." The door opened, and Krista enveloped Megan in a warm embrace. "I was about to call you. Did you come to see Ford? Oh, I'm so glad."

She drew Megan into the kitchen. Through the long hall Megan could see Krista's suitcases by the front door. Krista's worried blue eyes followed hers.

"Oh, the suitcases. You see, I was just leaving—I've really got to go. The taxi will be here any minute. But I do so hate leaving him alone just yet. And he's in such a mood. He can be such a dragon, sometimes, and his temper is particularly foul right now. I'm sure his arm is hurting terribly."

A horn sounded out front, and Krista frowned. "You see? The cab is here already. But if I don't hurry, I'll miss my plane, and when I asked him if he wanted me to stay a few more days, he just roared at me. See what you can do, won't you?"

Megan banished a cowardly impulse to run. "Well, I'll try," she said doubtfully, looking toward the sweep of the staircase as though she expected the "dragon" to come roaring down it at any minute. "Did he say he'd be willing to see me?"

"Willing?" Krista grabbed up a vanity case and hurried toward the front door. "What do you mean, willing? I'm sure he'll be thrilled. Well—" she grinned "—maybe not thrilled. He's feeling too grumpy right now for that, but I know you'll bring him out of it. You two seem to understand each other."

At the door Krista turned around, a shy smile on her face. "Megan—I hope we'll be seeing a lot of each other from now on. With you and Ford practically in business together—well, I just hope things work out. I know it's complicated. So much is happening now—" her grin became mysterious "—but I promised Ford he could tell you. But remember I hope we'll be good friends."

Her knowing smile was almost too blatant, and Megan could all too easily guess what caused it. Krista and Ford must have reached some kind of an arrangement— an official engagegement? But why was that complicated, and why would Krista want Ford to break it to Megan? Her breath caught. Was it possible that Ford had confessed that a perverse attraction had once existed between him and Megan? If so Krista was taking it well. Ford must have reassured her that Megan was no longer a threat.

Her heart hung like a hot stone in her chest, but she put a bright smile on her lips.

"Thanks, Krista. I'm sure we will," she said. In spite of her own misery, she wished she could take the strain from Krista's face. She really did like her so much.

"You catch your plane now and don't worry about anything down here. I promise you, he'll be back in New York as soon as he's strong enough to travel."

Krista smiled and gave Megan another impulsive hug before disappearing down the steps to the waiting taxi.

When she was gone, Megan stood for a long time at the foot of the stairs, trying to gather her courage. She couldn't go up there with despair written all over her face. In a way it was like the old days, when she had stood at the bottom of these same stairs, trying to arrange her features into a cheerful smile so Natalie wouldn't guess how dismal the doctor's report had been.

This time, though, it was Megan herself who'd been given the cruel diagnosis. If Ford was going to marry Krista, then this love that had come to her unbidden, unwanted, like a seed blown by an indifferent wind, would never grow. It'd had its one blossom, that one night when she had lain in his arms and felt the flowering, and that was all it would ever have.

She slid her hand across the bannister as she began her ascent. She wanted nothing more right now than to run, far and fast. But because she did love Ford, and because Krista was her sister, she would have to wish them happiness. Her nostrils flared with her effort to hold a smile in place. *Thank you, best wishes, I'm sorry, and good-*

bye. Hard phrases, all of them. But the last would be the worst.

At first she thought he was sleeping, and she stood in the doorway watching him, her heart beating erratically at the walls of her chest. His face was turned away from her, toward the window, where the magnolia tree's glossy leaves swished against the glass.

He lay above the covers, his magnificent body stretching from headboard to footboard. He wore only a faded pair of blue jeans, no shirt, and his heavily muscled chest was as tanned as molasses against the soft white spread. One arm was flung up across his brow as though to block out the light, and the other—her heart stumbled. The other was encased in white plaster, the fingertips dangling from the end of the cast.

A jumble of emotions washed over her—incongruous, intense emotions like awe and desire, gratitude and pity—and she had to brace herself to keep from tumbling under the force of them.

Apparently sensing her presence, he turned away from the window and blinked toward her, as though his eyes had been looking too long at the light.

"Kris?"

"It's Megan," she said thickly and moved in closer. "Krista had to leave."

Now that his face was turned to hers, she saw the marks his ordeal had left—the cuts, the scrapes, the ugly blue bruise above his right eye.

"Oh, Ford!" she exclaimed without thinking. "Your face! Does it hurt?"

"Only when I laugh," he said, smiling bitterly with the one undamaged corner of his mouth. "But that's not much of a problem today. I haven't been laughing much."

Instinctively she moved into the room, her eyes searching his lean face, assessing the damage. Though not serious still it looked painful. She longed to reach out and soothe those angry scratches, to kiss the—

Suddenly she drew back, her lungs pulling in air hard enough to make her head swim. Her eyes had snapped on the one mark that hadn't been left by the fire. There, on the clear, hard jut of his right cheekbone, was the unmistakable pink impression of a small kiss. Her mind's eye flashed to the scene downstairs of just moments ago—Krista's ladylike pink smile . . .

Megan put her hands behind her back. The kiss was like a brand, a flag of possession, warning her to stay back.

"I heard the news this morning," he went on. "Becky telephoned and told Krista. I should congratulate you. You won."

Megan didn't know what to say. It was the moment she'd been waiting for, working toward for two months . . . and still she felt no sense of victory. Instead she felt only the dull ache of longing that she had come to know so well.

"I know." It was all she could manage, and the dead sound of her voice was apparent even to him.

"Is that all? Just 'I know'?" He arched one brow. "Megan, you surprise me. I was prepared for a bit more swagger. Nothing ostentatious, just a little healthy pride in having bested me."

She shook her head. Passing the foot of the bed, she went to the window and fiddled with the silk curtains.

"How can I be proud?" She stared out the window at the tree. "It was Mr. Hamilton's cigar—did they tell you that? He must have left it burning." She turned her head slightly, just enough to see, out of the corner of her eye, his figure on the bed. "When he came to the open house I knew it wasn't wise to let him smoke in there. But I didn't dare risk offending him, so I didn't mention it. All I cared about was his money, the stupid bet."

Tears were piling up in her eyes, and she turned away again. To her blurred vision the swaying tree made a strange kaleidoscope of green and blue. And then the tears fell, clearing her vision as they trickled down her cheeks.

"So how can I be proud?" She lifted her chin, and the tears slid down across her throat and disappeared into the collar of her sweater. In spite of the evidence of her weakness, though, her voice was rough. "How can I be? It's all gone. Everything. And to a great extent, it's my fault."

A muffled curse sounded from the bed behind her, followed by an awkward rustling. She turned to see him struggling to sit up, his face contorted from the painful effort.

"Ford, don't," she said, reaching out to press him back toward the bed. "Don't try to sit up."

He subsided with a groan. "Then don't stand here and talk such damned nonsense," he growled, but his voice was laced with pain, and she realized that the broken arm was only the most visible of his injuries. The refectory table was so heavy—her heart seemed to stumble as she pictured him lying beneath it, unconscious as the smoke swirled around him.

As if of its own volition, her hand brushed his damp forehead, pushing the thick silk of his hair away. A "dragon"? Perhaps he seemed so to Krista, but Megan felt no fear. Even when he growled, his voice seemed to slide into some secret place inside her.

And he was definitely growling now. "That pompous fool, Hamilton, should have known better. You've got No Smoking signs posted, and any smoker knows enough to make sure the stubs are completely extinguished. Damn fool." Reaching up with his good hand, he grabbed her wrist, locking it inside his strong fingers. "Don't you dare blame yourself."

Wriggling her hand, she gently extricated herself and backed away. She had to. In another second he would have felt her pulse wildly fluttering against his fingers.

"Well, all that isn't important now," she said briskly, averting her gray eyes from his piercing green ones. The pain seemed to have brightened his eyes, leaving the whites glistening and the pupils dilated, and she couldn't look into them. "I didn't come to tell you my troubles. I really came to thank you. I know you tried to save the diary. You shouldn't have risked it, but I wanted you to know I'm very grateful."

He made a sound dangerously like a snarl. "Grateful?" he mocked her. "For what? I didn't get to the diary. In fact, I didn't manage to save even one pitiful scrap of paper. Not even a postcard. You've got nothing to be grateful for."

She folded her arms across her chest, as if to prevent his angry barbs from penetrating. "I am, though," she said mildly, refusing to enter into his bitter mood. "It was very brave and very generous of you to try—"

He cut her off with a curse. Breathing heavily, he raised himself to a half-sitting position and glared at her. "Stop it!" His hair had spilled again onto his forehead, and the muscles in his chest were thick with exertion. "You once accused me of patronizing you—well, dammit, don't start patronizing me now! Brave and generous? God, what awful words!"

"I'm sorry." She *was* sorry. She was still making such a mess of all this. But he seemed so angry. She didn't know what she could say that wouldn't elicit equally mocking responses.

So she decided to leave. Slowly she edged toward the door, though she had to force her feet to make the motions. They seemed to want to stay, to walk back to his side.

"I'll let you rest, then. We can talk about Memory Lane tomorrow, about what you're going to do—"

"There's nothing to talk about," he snapped. "You're going to take the insurance money and restock. The policy I bought covers one hundred percent of replacement costs. I know—you can't actually replace any of those things, but there must be other old things you can acquire. Do so."

She shook her head. "No, I don't think I can," she said wanly. "I don't think we can technically say I *did* win the bet. Remember, you stipulated that the inventory had to remain intact. And I hardly have the same value in inventory now that I had two months ago." She tried to smile. "Unless the price of ashes has gone up considerably since I last checked."

She had passed the bed again now, this time on her way out, and he was backlit, the bright daylight that streamed in through the big window throwing a shadow over his face. She could just barely glimpse the flash in his eyes.

"But as I said, we should talk about this tomorrow," she finished placatingly. No need to get into all of it now, when he was obviously in pain. "Or whenever you feel better."

She couldn't see the glint at all now, but she didn't have to—his tone was as cold as ice. "And as *I* said, there is nothing to talk about. Listen, Megan. You may have forgotten hearing the cathedral bells chime last night, but I haven't. That fire didn't start until *after* midnight. Our bet was over."

No, she hadn't forgotten the church bells. The whole night was etched into her memory forever.

"Well, we'll see." She knew the words sounded absurd—the meaningless, noncommittal words you might use to hush an importunate child—but since she couldn't speak the truth, those were the only words that came to her befuddled mind.

She couldn't tell him that suddenly she knew it was impossible for her to continue working for him, impossible for her to stay here at all. When he left for New York to pick up the life he had left, the life that would undoubtedly begin with a huge society wedding to Krista Kelly, Megan would not be able to endure the memories here in New Orleans.

Little things would be torment to her. The simple act of tallying up the days' receipts would remind her of him and these days of intense, intimate competition. The kiss of rain, the smell of smoke. He would be everywhere.

Never again would she be able to walk down the streets of the French Quarter without seeing Tony Ford's smile rising out of the mist. Never would she be able to hear a small child cry "Throw me something, Mister" without remembering his hard hands tenderly draping beads around her trembling neck.

Throw me something, Mister. The words had a terrible irony. If she stayed, she would always be waiting, hoping against hope that one night the lights would be shining in Natalie's windows, that a sleek black car would nudge into the driveway, that a low, urgent rap would echo in her midnight bedroom . . . *Throw me something, Mister.*

No, she couldn't live that way. She didn't want the crumbs of his life. She wouldn't settle for that. As horrible as the fire had been, it had given her the chance for a fresh start. The chains of the past, the chains of Natalie's will, Natalie's store, their own spiteful bet, these were the chains that had tied her to him—and the chains lay in ashes now. She must be strong enough to walk away.

Steel bands seemed to tighten around the hot column of her throat. But what of the other, softer chains? The chains of her love, her passion, her need? Those weren't as easily destroyed as the chains of the past.

"We'll see," she said again, stiffly. There really was nothing else that *could* be said.

From the doorway she allowed herself a last look. He had shifted to his side, was leaning on his one good elbow as he faced her at the door. But the effort had cost him. Moisture glistened on his skin, and the arm that held him was not as steady as it had been. His face, ordinarily so beautifully tanned, was strangely pale beneath his mahogany hair, and the bruises, the scratches, and yes, even the pink kiss mark, stood out vividly. His brows were drawn down hard over hollowed eyes, and the long, elegant ridge between cheekbone and jaw was deeper—too deep. His whole face was tensed with pain.

Oh, god, she thought, don't let him look so needy, so vulnerable. She groped for the doorknob. Thank you and I'm sorry had somehow been said. Now it was time for goodbye.

But his voice rang clear and cold into the room, stopping her feeble efforts. "And so that's it? You're leaving? Dammit, Megan, I think you owe me more honesty than this. I think you owe it to yourself."

His voice was as strained as his face, and her eyes flew to his.

"What do you mean?"

"I mean you ought to have the courage to tell me the truth. You're not planning to help rebuild Memory Lane, are you?"

Her mouth fell open slightly, and she stared into his blazing eyes helplessly. "I—I don't know..." she said, stumbling over the words.

"Oh, yes, you do," he shot back. "You're planning to walk out that door right now, and you're not ever coming back. I can hear it. I can feel it. I can see it in your eyes."

She dropped her gaze, self-conscious.

"And I know why you're going to do it."

Her head snapped up. "You do?"

He leaned his head back against the headboard, shutting his eyes as though the effort to hold them open had wearied him. "Of course. You made your feelings clear last night. It's a neat little impenetrable package. You hate Patrick Kelly. I'm the same kind of man as Patrick Kelly. Ergo—you hate me."

He opened his eyes, and even in the shadow thrown by the bright light she could see them flashing. "Oversimplified maybe, but I've caught the essential logic, haven't I?"

What kind of answer was there to such a question? He was, as he put it, essentially accurate. But it left out so much—it was so cold-blooded . . .

"Not exactly," she equivocated.

"Yes, exactly." His tone was unyielding. "But your facts are wrong. Your whole emotional logic is based on bad facts."

"Really?" She stiffened. She could hear it coming— the defense of Patrick Kelly, the attack on her mother. "I don't think it matters anymore. Let's forget it."

He shifted, groaning as the bruises and sprains bit into him. "No. I won't let it be that easy. You need to hear this."

"I don't want to hear anything that makes Patrick Kelly out to be an angel," she retorted angrily. "And I'm certainly not interested in listening to you paint my mother as a devil."

He was shaking his head. "Can't you *hear* yourself? Angels and devils? Dammit, Megan, don't you even remember what you told me the other night? You said the world wasn't all black and white. You said it was frightening shades of gray."

She bowed her head guiltily, remembering. It was true, she had said that. And she had meant it. But this was different.

"You helped me that night, Megan. You helped me to let go of an anger that had eaten away at me for most of my life. It was a wonderful, freeing feeling. Now I want *you* to listen."

She wanted to storm away, but she couldn't. If there was anything he could say...

"I'm sorry about the things I said last night, Megan. You were right to be angry. I didn't think—I just reacted. Your story was so incredible to me. I couldn't believe that I could have been wrong about Patrick."

His eyes roamed her face. "But I was just closing my eyes to the truth," he said finally. "And as soon as you'd gone I knew what a mistake I'd made. You're very much like him, you know. Much more so than Krista."

"Am I?" Her voice was small, but she heard the eager note she wasn't able to hide.

"Yes, you are." Ford must have heard it, too—there was a gentleness in his voice. "Patrick's hair wasn't as dark as yours, but it curled in the very same way, in huge, tempestuous circles. He wore it rather longer than most men his age, because he was proud of it."

Megan lowered her head, feeling those very curls tumbling across her shoulders to her cheeks. Against her will, she began to build a mental picture of her father, and something in her chest began to ache, as though a frozen part of her was beginning painfully to thaw.

"And his eyes..." Ford's voice was softer now. "His eyes were the same clear gray. Big, like yours, too. And they were changeable, like yours. Flashing, defiant in business. Wide and tender with his family."

Megan closed her eyes. She was looking inside now, not out.

"But what should have been the most obvious was the passion. He was a passionate man, Megan. When he loved, he loved fiercely. He loved Krista fiercely. Maybe he loved your mother, too."

Megan lifted pain-filled eyes to his. "Then *why*? Why didn't he ever write to her? Call her? *Anything!*" The thaw had created a flood, and her eyes were spilling the overflow. "Tell me that, if you know so much."

"I can't," he said softly. "I only know that he wasn't a monster. He was just a man. He made mistakes. But you've seen Felicia, seen how difficult she is. It must have been an act of great courage for him to send money to your mother at all. Given that he already had a difficult wife and a daughter he adored, there was no easy answer for him. But I imagine he thought he was doing the best he could for all of you."

She turned toward the door, a muffled cry of frustration escaping her. Though she knew he was right, that wasn't enough. She wanted to *know*. She needed to know. She was like a child again. She wanted to believe that her mother had meant something to this Patrick Kelly. She needed to know because—

The truth was like a sudden, blinding light. It wasn't because she needed to be assured that Patrick Kelly had loved her mother. That issue was long gone and had died with the two of them. No, she just wanted to believe that history wasn't simply, tragically repeating itself. She wanted to believe that *she* might have meant something to Ford Chadbourne, something more than a momentary passion.

"Meggie." His voice was like a caress, and she turned around slowly. "Look at me. This isn't really about Kelly, is it?"

She shook her head mutely. Why deny it? In some peculiar way, Ford Chadbourne was able to see into her heart. He had done it that first week, when he was just her charming Tony Ford, and he could do it still.

"I didn't think so. What *is* it, then? Why are you crying?" He patted the bed. "Come over here. Tell me."

Again she shook her head. Even through the watery curtain of her tears she could see the pink circlet left from Krista's kiss.

"Meggie, come!" His voice was impatient. "It hurts too much to get up and wrestle you over here. Don't make me do it."

"I mustn't...."

"Yes, dammit, you must!" He sounded furious and began making movements to rise.

His face twisted, and so did her heart. Quickly she let go of the door and dropped onto the bed, just beyond his reach.

"I'm here," she said soothingly. "Sit back."

"It's about time," he said, settling against the pillows with a sigh. "Now. Why the devil can't you just let go of the past, Meggie? Let it *be* the past! All those things happened to other people, and they mustn't be allowed to come between us now."

"I know that," she said humbly. And she was surprised to find that it was true. Natalie, Patrick—none of them mattered anymore. But the pink kiss was not the past. It definitely was the present. It probably was the future. Ford's future.

"Well? Then why don't you come over here and kiss me?"

She looked into his teasing eyes. How could he be so flippant? Didn't he know her well enough yet to realize she wouldn't be content to be his mistress?

"Because someone else got there first. I can't just be your—your..."

He looked bewildered. "What?" He squinted, tilting his head to study her, as though her face would hold the answer to the puzzle of her words. "Who got here first?"

"Krista did," she said quietly and reached out her finger to touch the pink circle. "And that's okay, Ford. She's a wonderful person. She'll make a terrific wife." She tried to keep the pain out of her voice. "But I would make a terrible mistress, Ford. I could never settle for that, not from anybody. But especially not from you."

There it was said. Now it was time to honor those proud words, to stand up and walk away.

But shockingly, Ford was smiling. Anger burgeoned inside her, and her cheeks flamed. He still thought it was funny?

"You're right on every count," he said, an undercurrent of laughter running through his voice. "You would make a terrible mistress. And Krista will make a wonderful wife."

As breathless as if he had struck her, Megan started to rise, but he flicked his hand out and caught her wrist. "But not *mine*," he added with steely emphasis, his voice finally serious.

Megan frowned at him, bewildered by the fast-moving currents of the conversation, afraid to believe what he seemed to be saying.

Grinning, he reached over to pick up Natalie's hand mirror from the nightstand and studied his face in the glass.

When he looked back at her, his eyes were sparkling. "Look at that, Meggie," he said, his voice low. "Light. Pink. Chastely applied to the cheek. *Not* the mark of my future wife."

His burning green eyes seemed to bore through her, and she felt a fire start low, deep within her.

"I've already been marked by the woman I want for my wife," he said, his voice dropping even lower. A tingle ran along her spine, bursting finally in a shiver that rippled across her collarbone and up into her hair.

"A woman with lips as red as fire. She kissed me here." He pulled her hand up to rest her fingertips against his lips. "But she left her mark on my heart."

He tugged harder at her hand, until she was off balanced, and had to fall to one elbow. "She's a woman with passion," he continued in the same, heart-melting tones, "a passion for life. For beauty. And for me."

His smile was blinding. "And not necessarily in that order."

She wasn't sure she could speak. Her heart was pounding in her throat, and she couldn't even swallow.

"But what about Krista—does she know, Ford? Will she . . . isn't she in love with you?"

He laughed. "Good grief—is that what you're worried about? I would have thought a woman of your passion would know the difference between friendship and love. Have you ever seen Krista look at me the way you're looking at me now?"

She glanced down quickly, embarrassed. Was it so obvious, then?

He chuckled and nudged her cheek with his hand. A sunburst of heat flamed out from the point of contact, and she leaned into his knuckle, instinctively seeking to prolong the contact.

"No, Meggie. Krista doesn't mind having me for a substitute brother—or a brother-in-law—but she wouldn't have me for a husband if I were the last man on earth. She thinks I'm . . . terrifying."

Finally Megan laughed, too. "A dragon—she told me today . . ."

"You see?" He shook his head, and the mahogany strands of hair gleamed in the bright afternoon light. "No, my scrupulous little Meggie. In spite of Felicia's best efforts, Krista just couldn't fall in love with me. Though, like a good daughter, she certainly tried. I tried, too. Krista and I are good friends, and for a while we even thought we might make it work somehow. Krista didn't have the nerve to defy her mother and I . . . well, I had just about decided I wasn't ever going to fall in love. . . ."

He touched her cheek gently. "And then I met you."

Megan bit her lip, still afraid to believe. "Then why did she come to New Orleans?"

He chuckled. "Felicia's no fool. One look at you, and she knew her plans were in serious danger. And then to hear we were in New Orleans, alone together! She must have been livid. So she flew Krista down for one last campaign. But Krista saw in no time how things really stood between you and me."

"Did she mind?"

"Lord, no!" He shook his head in mock disappointment. "She couldn't have been more relieved."

Megan bit her lower lip. It couldn't be true—how could any woman be *glad* to hear that Ford did not love her? It had nearly broken Megan's heart to think it. And yet it must be true. She remembered Krista's indifference to Ford's touch. . . . Amazing. And someday, would she and Krista talk about all this? Someday, when they could finally speak of their kinship? She felt a smile beginning deep within her. Perhaps. Perhaps someday.

But Ford was growing impatient. As if sensing her wandering thoughts, he slid his hand up from her elbow to her shoulder and pulled. Her arms gave way beneath her, so that her head dipped low, toward his naked chest. Her hair spilled black against the golden-brown skin, and she could feel his heat rising toward her.

"That's enough about them," he growled. "At the moment, I'm more concerned about you." Now that she was close enough, he fumbled with the buttons of her sweater, his one hand awkward. "What about you, Meggie? Do you think I'm a terrifying dragon?"

She smiled. "Not right now." She looked down at his hard fingers, hopelessly tangled in the fabric. "I'm not sure dragons can rear back and breathe fire if they're all bound up in plaster."

His fingers closed over the hem of her sweater in a ferocious fist, and he dragged her to him, his eyes as fiery as any dragon's.

"Oh, can't they?" He wrapped his hand hard behind her hair and smothered her mouth and her answering words with his lips. She tried to pull back, anxious in case he bruised his damaged face further, but he held her fast, apparently unaware of pain.

After a long moment he pulled back and smiled crookedly.

"See? I love you, Megan Farrell. Marry me," he whispered, "and I'll show you how hot the fire can be."

Her own smile was shaky, fragile, as though the muscles of her mouth had been weakened by the assault. But it was a wonderful weakness, and she was dizzy with the joy of being in his arms. She moved trembling hands to the buttons he had not been able to open.

"Show me first," she whispered. "And I'll marry you later."

Harlequin Presents

Coming Next Month

Available in June wherever paperback books are sold, or through Harlequin Reader Service:

In the U.S.
901 Fuhrmann Blvd.
P.O. Box 1397
Buffalo, N.Y 14240-1397

In Canada
P.O. Box 603
Fort Erie, Ontario
L2A 5X3

Indulge a Little
Give a Lot

A LITTLE SELF-INDULGENCE CAN DO
A WORLD OF GOOD!

Last fall readers indulged themselves with fine romance and free gifts during the Harlequin®/ Silhouette® "Indulge A Little—Give A Lot" promotion. For every specially marked book purchased, 5¢ was donated by Harlequin/ Silhouette to Big Brothers/Big Sisters Programs and Services in the United States and Canada. We are pleased to announce that your participation in this unique promotion resulted in a total contribution of *$100,000.*

*

Watch for details on Harlequin® and Silhouette®'s next exciting promotion in September.

BIG BROTHERS/BIG SISTERS AND HARLEQUIN

Harlequin is proud to announce its official sponsorship of Big Brothers/Big Sisters of America. Look for this poster in your local Big Brothers/Big Sisters agency or call them to get one in your favorite bookstore. Love is all about sharing.

Have You Ever Wondered If You Could Write A Harlequin Novel?

Here's great news—Harlequin is offering a series of cassette tapes to help you do just that. Written by Harlequin editors, these tapes give practical advice on how to make your characters—and your story—come alive. There's a tape for each contemporary romance series Harlequin publishes.

Mail order only

All sales final